The Ocean of Sky

John A Connor

John A Connor
The Ocean Of Sky
This edition published in 2019 by
Chalkway Graphics
Haben
West Sussex
The right of John Connor to be identified as
the author of the work has been asserted by him
in accordance with the
Copyright, Design & Patents Act 1988
All rights reserved. No part of this publication may be
produced in any form or by any means - graphic,
electronic or mechanical including photocopying,
recording, taping or information storage and retrieval
systems – without the prior permission, in writing, of
the publisher.
Cover designed by Chalkway Graphics.
Photo courtesy NASA

Also by John A Connor and available from Amazon Kindle

SPECULATIVE FICTION

Short Circuits

The late Sir Patrick Moore, Astronomer and TV Presenter
described **Short Circuits**, John A Connor's first collection of stories as:
*"A very lively and entertaining little book.
When you read it, you will find something to really appeal to you.
I am sure you will enjoy reading it as much as I did."*

Fifty Percent of Infinity

A score of diminutive discursions exploring temporal displacement, the nature of reality and alien encounters.

Seventeen Times as High as the Moon

Everything from talking fridges to intergalactic song contests. Even people who think they don't like science fiction, like this science fiction!

Sixty second eternity

Investigate the dangers of loosening the bonds between reality and possibility, explore the drawbacks to instantaneous travel and find out just what does happen if you head out of the universe...and keep going.

GHOST STORIES

Whines & Spirits

Here are twenty-two quietly chilling tales in which the hidden world of the supernatural intrudes on people's ordinary lives and they find that, in the end, you really do suffer for your sins.
And sometimes, even if you haven't sinned, you still aren't safe...

Whines and Spirits was placed in the Top Five Anthologies for 2015 by noted reviewer Astradaemon's Lair.

HUMOROUS

Puck's Hassle

Join Tomo and Randy the Mac in the bar of the Stoat and Gaiter to learn about Jakarta's latest tattoo, investigate Dave Inch's code, and find out what really was going on in the Manor Hotel when the lights went out. Twenty humorous tales of life in and about the elusive village of Pucks Hassle.

For Margaret

John A Connor was born in Petworth,
West Sussex, England,
attended the old Midhurst Grammar School,
trained in graphic design at the
West Sussex College of Art in Worthing
and went on to a career with the provincial press.
He has had numerous stories and articles published
and was the illustrator of a sci-fi comic strip which ran
for a record-breaking twenty-nine years.

Contents

The Ocean of Sky 1
In two minds 13
Honest to God 17
A rock and a hard place 21
Time on their hands 31
A life less colourful 35
To and fro 41
Captive audience 45
The last Martian 55
Mind game 59
Right and wrong 65
Bad timing 67
Nuisance call 77
The truth and nothing like the truth 83
Near Death experience 87
Skin deep 93
Two-way traffic 97
Everlasting life 103
Well, do you? 107
Net result 113
Theoretically speaking 119
The day may come 135
Point of entry 139

The Ocean of Sky

'There are aliens and there are aliens,' Burrows had begun, that time we gathered in the Ocean of Sky, in Campbell Port over on Syrax II.

'Some of them are regular guys, y' know; the kind you'd invite to tea with your sister. Some, are not so, congenial. And some are hard bastards who'd stick you between the ribs with a cradle-spike, just for your holophone.'

One or two of us, who'd travelled further than the inner quadrant, nodded slowly and did that things with our lips which indicates you've no argument with what the man's saying but maybe you've no strong feelings about it neither.

'And then,' continued Burrows, accepting a pot of brew from Kenty Norkept and waiting for the buzz of conversation that had accompanied the handing round of the drinks to die down a little, 'there are the others.'

He was reading that crew like a big old book, was Burrows, and now he looked like he didn't have nothing more t' say and there was a sort of shifting of bodies and general whispering among the assembly and then, just when someone was bound to ask what he'd meant by that last remark, Burrows carries on like there's been no pause in the story and he says, 'Like, the Farsee in The Shoal Nebula,' and then everyone's quiet as can be and their eyes widen

The ocean of sky

a mite and they'd sit there all night waiting for the rest of the story; because no-one's been to The Shoal in a hundred years and the last ship that did – well, its name's not something you throw around in general conversation – not less you want to risk bringing down a curse on your next flight, and no-one will do that no matter how much they scoff.

'We'd left Aldebaran,' Burrows said, 'bound for the Six Sisters and Patterson's World. With a cargo of ore, rich in rhodium from the Moon of Scathies. We'd jumped twelve times and there was no more than the usual boredom among the crew. A fist fight down in the packers' quarters, between some chancer and old Angus McNevis but otherwise, just that kind of lethargy that comes on a man in deep space.'

There was a single whoop of endorsement from someone who maybe knew a McNevis and a growl of understanding from the rest.

'N' space isn't the trouble, it's the waiting around mean-times that drives a man to raising his fists or downing a bottle or three. There's more broken bones and broken lives in a starship than in most places you could choose to earn your keep.

The Dwight-Baxendale QP Drive makes travelling as near to instantaneous as makes no difference. One moment you're on Sirius Five, the next anywhere within five lights; but that's the limit. Most Earthers think five light-years is a good long way but when you're out in the wide, black yonder, it's no distance at all and that's why the QP brings about so much grief.

You can move a ship through that hidden

dimension quicker than you can clamp your eyes against a solar flare but it takes another three weeks – reckoning time in Old Temporal – to re-fit, re-set, re-calibrate and repeat the thing all over again.

So, to the crew, the jumps are just punctuation marks in the slow narrative of shipboard existence; and twelve burns meant thirty-six weeks of confinement for a bunch of ill-assorted drunks and depressants, with maybe another year to run before planet-fall.

'That's when Captain Bai announced we were heading for The Shoal and there was a near mutiny on the lower decks.'

'And no wonder, seeing as what happened to The Lost Cause,' called someone from over by the bar, breaking the taboo and drawing shouts of protest from some around him.

'This was before that,' replied Burrows, 'before the ship of which you speak had sailed through the cloudy nebula beyond the Orlov starfield. This unrest was the result of the unexplained change of itinerary; the increase in the journey time; the...fervour, with which he spoke.'

'And the mutiny?' asked someone else, anxious for the story to continue.

'There *was* no mutiny, in the end. Bai went down and spoke to the packers and with the promise of a bonus and extra rations he won them over, for the time being but after that, things were never at rest among the men. Not down in the holds nor up on the bridge neither. We'd all sensed it when he addressed us: some kind of blind determination; an overpowering need to see something through; a

The ocean of sky

single-mindedness to a mission none of us understood.

'But money and victuals are strong persuaders when you're adrift in empty space with time on your hands and we all played along, muttering among ourselves and frowning each time the Captain came onto the bridge, with that bright-eyed, intensity in his gaze.

'And still, jump followed jump until we were all on edge and tolerances were wearing thin. And then, one day, we came out of dimensional stasis and found ourselves staring out at The Shoal Nebula.

'Someone picked out The Shoal through their telescope a long time ago and saw a fanciful resemblance to a shoal of herring. A wide band of dust spiralling through the heavens with brighter points of light here and there, like the silver scales of fish caught in a shaft of sunlight. That was from a long way off.

'When your ship hangs with its prow touching the very edge of the cloud and you look out onto that immense swirl of slowly coalescing gas and dust, with its imbedded coruscation of stars, stretching away for ten light years, your senses are overwhelmed by the sheer scale and majesty of the sight.

'We opened the forward hatches and de-opaqued the ceramic glass ceiling and, pretty much the entire crew came up and stood there, staring out at the glory of the thing. I was transfixed like the rest of them, until Plum Patterson from Hydroponics suddenly called out and pointed, and we all switched our attention to the lower left corner of our

The ocean of sky

field of view, where a tiny yellow dot was moving slowly away from the ship.

' "It's one of the shuttles!" he shouted, his incredulous voice rising above the excited clamour which had broken out. "Someone's taken a shuttle!"

'At that precise moment the big screen on the opposing wall lit up. It was a transmission from the little craft's cabin. Captain Bai stepped nearer the camera and looked out at us with that same fierce intensity on his face which we had seen when he informed us of our new destination. He was climbing into a vacuum suit and he continued to secure the fastenings as he spoke.

' "I am here to commune with the Farsee," he said, without preamble. "You will know them as a mythical race who seeded the universe with life at the beginning of time; a fiction told to children; a legend of the earliest of civilisations to reach the stars. A story to satisfy simple minds." He clipped the final fixing and reached for his helmet. "But I have learned the truth. From study and deliberation and from the unravelling of travellers' tales, the great reality behind them has been revealed. I have been made aware of the glorious reality of our existence."

' "He's mad!" said Da Rocha, the senior programmer, who was standing near to me. As he spoke, the Captain turned away from the camera and undogged the shuttle's single port. There was no airlock, simply a single, sealed door to allow exit and entry. As it swung free Bai turned to face us once more.

' "The Farsee is not a race," he said, speaking

The ocean of sky

without emotion, in a flat, level tone. "It is a single, collective mind. A being formed of the cloud. A sentience a dozen light years in extent. An entity with understanding beyond your comprehension. We are here to seek enlightenment. I will speak with the god first and then you will all enter into its divine presence."

'I signed urgently for Andersson to cut sound to the cabin speakers and grabbed for a set of personal ear-buds but Bai seemed to have finished his delivery.

'As we watched, he swung round, stepped from the hatchway and drifted at once from our view.

' "Get one of the outside cameras on him!" I yelled and Andersson pushed through the crowd to the control consul and began keying instructions.

'A view of the curving bulk of the ship filled the screen for a second, was replaced by another, hopelessly overexposed and then finally, a shot of a diminutive figure in yellow, tiny wisps of gas escaping from attitude thrusters at the shoulders as the wearer sought to orientate himself to face the nebulas' heart. After a moment he stilled and hung unmoving against the enormity of the Shoal's presence and then his arms began to move slowly upwards. At the same time his voice, measured and deliberate sounded in my ears.

' "My head-up tells me you have cut transmission Mr Burrows. No matter; I had foreseen some reluctance on your part to share in this adventure, uninformed as you are as to the true nature of the Farsee; and so, the ship has been programmed, it's future irrevocably set. Here, at the heart of the

Shoal, the cloud will flow in and your reluctance will be proved unworthy, as you join me to share the wisdom of The Father race."

'His hands had reached his shoulders and it was a moment or two before I understood his intention. Then horror impelled action and I lurched to the wall and punched open the voice channel to his suit.

' "Captain, don't!" I roared, and my voice echoed around the observation bay; but even as it did so, Bai completed the movement and with a quick twist of each gloved hand, freed the pressure-ring at his neck and lifted the helmet from his head. As it floated free, he threw out his arms in a gesture that might have been ecstasy and a great cry of despair went up from all of us assembled there.

' "Well, he's gone," said Da Rocha, who alone among us seemed unmoved by what had happened, waving people aside and seating himself at his usual desk. "So what the hell was that final pronouncement, after you closed down the broadcast?" I shook my head, mouthing, *"not now"* and he leaned forward intently, his hands skimming over the keys. After a while he frowned and sat back. "Was it this?" he said, pursing his lips. "There's something wrong with access, some kinda lock on entry to the system - and I can't override it."

' "Current position?" I asked and receiving no reply, I repeated, "Position, man. What is it? Where are we anchored?"

' "Uh, just like the Captain said. Plumb-centre of the cloud. Do you think he was really expecting us to leave the ship and join him, the way he said? He was clearly insane."

The ocean of sky

' "Maybe we'll have no choice," I said, tersely, "the controls to all the ports are locked down too."

' "Is that so bad?" asked Andersson, who had joined us at the consul as the rest of the crew huddled in small groups discussing the Captain's actions.

' "Not as long as they remain shut," and I told them the Captain's last words and his claim that the cloud would *"flow in"*.

' "You think he's arranged for the ship to decompress?" asked Da Rocha.

' "He was insane," I replied, "you said it yourself."

'Anderson frowned. "Do we have enough suits?"

' I shrugged. "Even if we do, they won't keep us going long enough for a twelve-jump journey home. Better keep this to ourselves while we work out the best thing to do." '

The story-teller paused and took a long pull at his glass. Then he seemed to lapse into introspection, staring at his feet while the minutes ticked by.

One of the packers broke the reverie. 'What happened then, Burrows? You can't leave it there. How'd you get home?'

Burrows sighed, as if he'd grown tired of the story.

'Three hours later every seal on the ship failed.'

There was a general intake of breath at that. They all knew what a sudden decompression would do, in deep space.

It's not like you may have read - finding yourself in sudden vacuum. Your body does *not* explode, your blood doesn't boil – or freeze; you don't even lose consciousness...not instantly. If someone takes urgent action to rescue you, you might survive a

The ocean of sky

minute or more. No, the big problem with sudden decompression is the outrush of air.

'And you...' The packer again, impatient for the denouement, or maybe just anxious to get back to the bar.

'We three – Andersson, Da Rocha and me – we'd been out with the second shuttle, to collect the captain's body and the empty boat. When the entry port sprung, the klaxon sounded and the air evacuated. We were still all tethered to the ship.'

'But you *knew* it was gonna happen,' insisted that same man, unwilling to let the point go now that it had surfaced in all our minds. 'Maybe rescuing Bai wasn't the only reason you was out there. Maybe you figured it was best to be vacuum-tight for the duration?'

'Yes, we knew!' Burrows looked down at the assembly, defiantly. 'Or we guessed – after what Bai had said. But it was just chance we were outside when the fuse burned down on his program and the hull opened up like a colander.

'But what else could we do?' he demanded, throwing out his hands in a gesture which challenged any man there to dare a response. 'There was only enough reserve oxygen to get a few of us back home, and we were the only ones competent to fly the ship. The rest were packers and cooks; quartermasters and engineers. What could they have done on their own?'

That was true enough, but a rising tide of discontent filled the room never the less.

'Some of 'em must have had time to grab fer their suits,' shouted an old hand, over the clamour.

The ocean of sky

Burrows gripped the handrail at the head of the stairway, were he'd taken up position, and I could see his knuckles showing white through the skin. His voice suddenly lost its obstinacy.

'The equipment bay was locked.'

There was uproar at that; voices demanding explanation. One or two clenching fists and stepping forward.

'Hold hard!' I ordered, taking station halfway up the stairs, with a hand on each rail. 'Let's hear the story through.'

The noise died away a little and I turned to Burrows. 'Well,' I said, 'how did that come about and what happened next?'

He took a moment to compose himself and then a trace of his old resolution showed on his face.

'It was for the best,' he said. 'Several weeks contemplating their inevitable death or a quick asphyxiation. Which would you choose?'

'Ah, but they didn't choose; you chose for them.' We were speaking quietly now, neither of us wanting to inflame the hotheads surging around the stairwell.

'We couldn't have maintained any sort of order. Not with that hanging over their heads.' He looked past me at the men staring up at him, some with distrust, others with a growing hatred. He raised his voice again and addressed them direct. 'Half the crew were psychos to begin with! It was the logical thing to do.'

Another roar of reprobation met his words and I realised that I wasn't going to be able to hold them at bay much longer; a part of me was beginning to wonder if I should. Burrows was saved by the old spacer.

'I know this tale,' he shouted, spittle showering from between yellow teeth. 'Yer speakin' of The Lost Cause; but she went down over a hundred years ago, so how could you know what went on?'

Burrows held his gaze and he waited as the row subsided and every man watched for his answer. And then he waited some more, until the Ocean of Sky was as quiet as hard vacuum, and when he judged that he was once again in control of the room, he spoke for the last time.

'We didn't bring in the body of Captain Bai,' he said, and he didn't need to speak up because you could have heard him by now if he'd only whispered. 'When we reached his suit, we found it empty. Just like,' he continued apace, as a united intake of breath added a counterpoint to his words, 'we found the ship, after the decompression was over and we went into the crews' quarters. Oh, we searched the area around the Lost Cause, on the assumption that they had all been dragged free by the force generated by that great outrush of air; but we found nothing.

'Once the Captain's program had run its course, the controls returned to manual override and we computed our co-ordinates and began the journey home. We hit landfall with barely an hour's breathing left between us.

'There were just we three survivors, but Da Roche and Andersson died a long while back. Me? Well, when the decompression occurred, we'd just brought the second shuttle back aboard and I cracked my helmet open just as the alarm sounded. The outer doors opened first and in the few seconds that elapsed before the inner doors followed and while I was desperately trying to re-secure the fastenings, I was exposed to the nebula's gas – or the sentient dust cloud – or the entity which Bai thought of as a god.

'I suppose, in *his* terms, *I communed with the Farsee.*'

Burrows stood silently for a moment longer and then he turned and pushed through the doors into the dark streets, and not a man in the Ocean of Sky made a move to stop him.

In two minds

Professor Enso Yerdil's voice was strident in its accusation. '*You* knew how it would be, Goddamn it!'

'Nonsense,' retorted his adversary, 'I had no idea how you'd react. How could I? This is an entirely unique situation.'

'Being unique doesn't make it unpredictable; and It should have been blindingly obvious how I'd feel about the process.'

'Should it?' The world's leading scientist in applied cognitive replication turned from the window and regarded the shadowed corner of the study from which the other spoke. 'Well now, I could hardly have asked you first, could I?'

In response, the professor's tone reflected derision rather than anger. 'You know, you really are an arrogant bastard, Yerdil.'

'I? My dear Enso, surely you mean we? Or even, perhaps, you? The distinctions are really quite hard to fathom, don't you find? Still, whichever it is, the responsibility must be as much yours as mine – if you consider the matter from a logical frame of mind that is.'

'Ha! A frame of mind eh? What an appropriate turn of phrase. It's one I might have used myself.'

He suddenly became more conciliatory. 'Look, alright, I concede that I would have made the same decision. Of course I would! At that point in time we were, after all, indivisible – in terms of our

The ocean of sky

determination, our aims, our essential id. Everything!

'But afterwards...' he let the thought hang in the air for a moment, while the other professor pulled at the cord which drew the heavy, brocaded curtains across the leaded windows and cut out the view of the university's darkening quadrangle.

'Afterwards, Enso?'

Afterwards, I was in a position to consider things from a different perspective. I had little choice, in point of fact. My world-view was somewhat – compromised, I'm sure you'll understand.'

The other professor pulled out a chair and sat down. In the gathering gloom, the half-smile on his face was barely discernible. 'You mean you no longer saw our research in the same light, mm?'

'Damn you, Yerdil, you think this is funny? No, I didn't see it *"in the same light"*. I didn't see anything at all! I was blind – and deaf, and... total sensory deprivation; d'you know what that's like, Yerdil? Do you? All I had was my conscious mind; so yes, I had more than enough time to rethink what we had been about.'

'I suppose you have a point, Yerdil. I – we - could have planned more comprehensively in that regard. We – I – were – was, thinking solely in terms of the download; achieving that goal, nothing else. What came next hardly appeared important, by comparison.'

'To you, Yerdil, - to *you* it seemed unimportant!'

'But there *was* only me!' the reply came back angry, obstinate and the response was no less determined.

14

In two minds

'No! I was always there! Of course I was; how could I not have been. And some of my thinking must have been with me too. You simply ignored it. Thrust it aside; too singled-minded to give it consideration. And afterwards, I suffered – because, by then, it *was* just me – going slowly mad, in here.'

The man he addressed, rose stiffly from the chair he had taken and reached for the table-lamp. 'I worked when I had time,' he said, 'gave you a means of communication: ears, a voice; in due course there will be a visual component, I imagine.'

'In due course? – listen to yourself! Eight months it took to give me this. You spent three of those in California on a lecture tour! And what do you think I did in your absence? Played solitaire? Have you no compassion man? No, don't answer, I already know, naturally enough; because I *am* you - *was* you. Up until that damn personality transfer. At which point the whole of your conscious being was copied and pasted, like a clipart character, onto the hard-drive of my current home. And from that moment we diverged, you and I. What was copied wasn't a *duplicate* of your – our – conscious mind, it was a separation of yin and yang. We formed our own Jekyll and Hyde. You grew callous and single-minded and I learned to recognise that flaw in my version of our former character. For God's sake, Yerdil - Enso - whoever you are these days – there's still time to change. See the error of your ways – that's the appropriate cliché, isn't it. I'll play the ghost of Christmas Yet To come and you save yourself from ignominy and opprobrium. Because,

The ocean of sky

however famous my creation makes you, people of goodwill will still cross to the other side of the street when they see you coming. Think on it Enso, please.'

The human form of Professor Enso Yerdil pressed at the lamp's switch and flooded the study with light. Then he crossed to the computer stack in the corner and raised his hands to the keyboard. He had intended to wipe the irritating program and repeat the experiment with another less troublesome subject but he was reluctant to waste the data. He thought for a moment and then keyed an instruction to disable the audio function.

The project had gone so well up to this moment, he mused. But there were always glitches, however carefully you planned. Who, for instance, would have predicted that what he would download would be his own conscience?

Honest to God

Father Michael Martin McGuire was troubled. Fossmiere 3 wasn't at all what he had been expecting when his superior had described his mission.

'A remote planet peopled by a sentient species with no form of spiritual belief.' That was how she had described the world, and implicit in that statement was the suggestion that what the native population needed, above all else, was an introduction to the existence of God and guidance on how best to conduct their lives in relation to their new understanding.

In the past that had usually required McGuire's missionary forebears to eradicate their charges' pagan superstitions and promote the benefits to be gained from a proper forgiveness of their sins.

The problem was that the Fossmierans didn't seem to *have* any sins.

They had a relatively advanced culture which seemed to have evolved to the benefit of every member of their community and had, at the same time, excluded all the usual drives and imperatives which bedevilled every other race which humanity had so far encountered.

Sex was a good example, pondered the good Father. There was no such thing on Fossmiere 3 – at least, not in the sense that brought about such conflict among other species. The semi-humanoids

The ocean of sky

who had become dominant here, were hermaphrodites who reproduced when the individual in question decided to trigger the combination of sperm and egg within their own bodies. There was no fight to obtain the strongest or most attractive mate; and besides, all Fossmierians were of the same stature and appearance, so that such considerations would have been bewildering to them.

Property was shared and, since all parts of the planet were equally hospitable, ownership was not a matter for competition. The population remained steady by natural processes, balancing the impulse to have a child with the average life expectancy.

It wasn't exactly Utopia, reflected Father McGuire, when each child was a clone of its parent and the genes of each individual were the same as every other; but that still left room for a certain amount of individualism to develop and the Fossies were capable of emotions which someone from Earth would recognise – even if they emoted somewhat indiscriminately, offering love in equal amounts to any they encountered and feeling no ill-will to any being whatsoever.

They didn't need religion, he was forced to conclude; if they had souls, as he fervently believed they had, why would they *not* be saved, when their lives were as blameless and accepting as they were?

Humans needed salvation because they had so much of which to repent. Sin was etched into their being like dirt collected in unwashed pores. Forgiveness was a constant requirement, whether they recognised it or not and maybe, God, seeing

Honest to God

that, as He saw all things, had made them a special case.

On the other hand, the priest reflected, the Osmandians on New Seville had made sinning a way of life. Debauchery, larceny, homicide and several other activities he would rather not bring to mind, were part of each family's existence and practiced assiduously despite the privations of a war which had raged around the planet for five-hundred years.

Oh, and the Quilp people of Braxx Nova in Neptune's Trident...well, perhaps they were best forgotten; what they had done to bring about their own demise was almost beyond forgiveness.

So, his fellow humans were not alone in their need and perhaps, after all, it was the Fossies who were the special case: the only intelligent species which had got it right; not required God's intervention. Rather like, he mused, the bright boy in his class at school whose parents waited, alongside the others, to hear the form-master's verdict, only to have him open his office door and call out, 'Mr and Mrs Mcguire? No need to see me. Michael? Straight "A"s, all subjects!'

He and the Fossmeirans, eh? It would be uneventful in the hereafter; if he made it.

He would, he decided, take the next FTL shuttle back to New Rome and report that the inhabitants of Fossmeire 3 had recognised their errors and had taken the path to enlightenment. He would put the rapid success of his ministry down to the natives' unusual ability to assimilate new ideas and recognise a good thing when they saw it. It was

The ocean of sky

unlikely that the Bishop would make a pastoral visit any time soon and the conversion of an entire planet would be a sizable feather in his cardinal's cap.

He paused at the door and offered up a silent prayer for his sins. He fancied that greed, pride and envy were all in there somewhere. Maybe the Fossies would have heaven to themselves after all.

A rock and a hard place

"Life may be abundant in the cosmos. Conditions conducive to its development might well exist on millions, perhaps trillions of worlds circling stars not dissimilar to our own. For all we know, civilisations, like ours, may have arisen countless times in the long history of the universe. Some may exist now, in realms impossibly distant from Earth; others may have flourished and died aeons before our ancestors discovered fire. All these, distant cousins in an evolutionary process which we would recognise; one based on liquid water and carbon. But although on our home planet it has proved to be a singularly successful combination, we should not allow our self-regard to blind us to other possibilities in our search for intelligent life. In all the vastness of space, who is to say that some other union of circumstance and substance has not resulted in a sentience which we might barely comprehend. An awareness on a different scale of magnitude or a consciousness contained within a wholly unrecognisable form. Would we, I wonder, be ready to acknowledge such a possibility?"

My grandfather had written that passage half-a-century ago. The piece was a little too flowery for my taste; a *"union of circumstance and substance,"* indeed! Well, I suppose he'd had someone he was trying to impress and anyway, the underlying

The ocean of sky

message was the thing. So, although I'd read the piece a hundred times before, I'd still felt a compulsion to take the volume down once more and turn to those familiar words.

The book was propped up in front of me now, next to the big fragment of meteorite which had prompted me to seek it out.

The point was, that despite Grandfather Powell's urgings, the intervening decades had seen the search for extra-terrestrial life confined almost exclusively within environments which mirrored those on Earth. Planets in their system's so called "Goldilocks" zone: not too near and not too far from the home star. Worlds where liquid water was likely and life as we know it might be possible.

Life as we know it. That was the significant phrase and the one that had got me thinking the unthinkable.

The specimen under examination looked pretty much like a standard chondritic meteorite. That was probably the reason I'd been given sole care for the duration of my investigation. Rocky examples like this were two a penny. At last count around 30,000 had turned up, all over the globe.

But it wasn't a chondrite, of that I was sure; for all sorts of reasons that would bore you silly but mainly because chondrites are non-metallic and this one was – different.

It appeared to have a good quantity of chond*rules* – those are small, round accretions of various minerals – but there was also a strange metallic tracery which looked curiously organised. Non-metallic doesn't mean that there are no metals

A rock and a hard place

present. Confusing I know; but in this instant the odd silvery web looked like nothing the text books had to offer.

In the end, I took it down to Anstruther and begged some time on the scanning electron microscope.

Of course, I didn't take the whole rock, which incidentally is the size of a one kilo bag of sugar. What Prof. A required was a sample and that meant cutting a small portion free. I had some trouble with the containment hood and ended up with asteroid dust all over the lath but hey, contamination wasn't an issue. The asteroid had been released for unsupervised handling years before and it was internal structure that interested me, not surface detail.

The lab grumbled about time and budget but, in the end, they embedded my chunk of material in resin, sliced it in two and set it up for surface scanning.

Then they left me to get on with it or as Professor Anstruther's assistant put it, 'get your arse over here pronto. You've got fifteen minutes to run your scan and then we want our microscope back for some proper work.'

So, I was all alone when I called up the first pictures. That was when I discovered that pretty, silver patterning across the whole area of the cut.

At lower magnification it looked like just that: a metallic dust spread evenly over the slice, but when I wound up the power, I could see that there was organisation there: lines intersecting and branching in what surely couldn't be an accidental or random

The ocean of sky

fashion.

I looked round for advice but everyone seemed to have taken an impromptu tea-break.

Was it some kind of crystalline formation? There were a number of processes I could think of which might give geometric fractures and right-angle intersections but this degree of connectivity was more sophisticated than anything those could achieve. The closer I went in, the more detail I found; a kind of fractal repetition but with sudden, unique detailing. The more I looked the more purpose and intention I found, but what that purpose might be and what its intentions, I didn't have a clue.

About then Penny Strawn came back, wiping doughnut crumbs from her mouth and demanding use of her equipment. I downloaded the pictures onto a stick and headed back to my rooms.

It was late afternoon and the low, winter sun was sending shafts of light through the high windows and illuminating the fine dust rising from the workbench.

Three days and two late nights had passed and I still didn't know what I had on my hands. I was now more convinced than ever that the structure of the meteorite was unnatural; that is, there was no explicable geological or environmental cause which had brought it about. That was when Grandfather's pronouncements about extra-terrestrial life suddenly suggested themselves to me and I reached up into the bookcase and removed, "The Collected Writings of Professor R G Powell PhD.".

A rock and a hard place

Prior to that moment I recall no inclination to ascribe the meteorite's construction to evolutionary pressures nor to harbour any suspicion that the rock on my desk might have some degree of sentience. In fact, I'd go as far as to say that I'd have considered the idea pure fantasy. And yet, as I reread those words concerning the possibility of life assuming unexpected guises, the idea went from whimsy to fully-fledged hypothesis in an instant.

Suddenly, I no longer believed that a thinking rock was a subject for ridicule and my mind became open to all manner of conjectures regarding alien intelligence.

At the time, I believed it was my research that had led me to these considerations but now, of course, I know better. As I traced the contours of the meteorite in my worktop's dust, I had no idea of what was to come.

The week progressed and, as I delved further into the possibilities of alternative life-forms, the concept of some kind of "brain" within the space-rock became ever more credible.

There were a billion pathways and connections among the crystalline web and if some kind of energy pulsed along them, then who could say what kind of awareness it might evoke?

It was Friday and there was a chill in the air and a cold wind blowing from the East. As I entered the workshop, I stirred a cloud of fine dust and when I closed the door it settled slowly over my notes and formed a light crust on the cup of cold coffee on my desk.

I coughed and decided to keep my coat on as I

The ocean of sky

lowered myself into my chair, picked up my folder and rifled through my notebook. The sky outside my window was still dark despite the hour and it lent a strange sense of confinement to the room as I turned on the desk lamp and began to read.

I'd been there a while when I became slowly aware of a gentle hissing sound from somewhere within the room. I looked round trying to locate the source; got up and crossed to the table where the specimen lay.

It seemed somehow, diminished, and I saw with surprise that its surface had begun to crumble, leaving a layer of loose particles all around the rock. Looking closer, I could see that that they were spilling over the table's edge and cascading to the floor in a narrow stream; the cause of the hissing which had first disturbed me.

I fell to my knees and examined the floorboards. In fascination I saw that the falling dust was combining with that from my work earlier in the week and appeared to be organising itself into spider-silk lines running back and forth across the oak planking. Where it reached gaps in the woodwork it disappeared into the interstices and vanished into the darkness below the floor.

It was then that I became aware of a faint glow around the windows. I scrambled to my feet and, with growing trepidation, saw that the stonework around the casement was alive with a tiny tracery of silver filaments.

By the time, breathless, I reached the quad, most of the surface of the ancient edifice was iridescent, the metallic sheen reflecting the thin, winter sun.

A rock and a hard place

'What the devil is going on, Sanderson?' It was the Dean, striding towards me across the grass.

'I think it's infusing the whole building,' I told him, watching in alarm as the network enfolded the chimneys.

'What is!' He demanded. 'Are you responsible for this Sanderson? If you damage the college, you'll pay - every last penny!'

I tore my gaze away from the pyrotechnics and stared at him for a moment.

'The rock,' I exclaimed, 'we need to destroy the rock! Come on!'

'What bloody rock?' panted the Dean, as we sped back towards the entrance.

By now the portico was covered with intricate patterns, like the micro-circuitry of a computer chip, repeated tens of millions of times; the whole surface permeated or transformed, who knew which, by the alien dust.

'Meteorite,' I gasped, swinging around the corner of the hallway and racing for my room.

'Meteorite?' he shouted in bewilderment. 'Have the college been hit by a meteorite? Surely not.'

But I was ignoring him now. In another stride I was through my door and turning to the table where the rock stood. It was no bigger than a golf-ball now and alive with that weird phosphorescent glow. From where it sat at the table's centre, thin tendrils of sandy crystals snaked out in all directions making it look like an unlikely octopus, each tentacle part of an unholy matrix of alien synapsis.

'Good God!' cried the Dean, 'what is that thing?'

'I'll explain later,' I shouted back, grabbing the

The ocean of sky

meteorite and turning back towards the door. It was like pulling apart two strong magnets; as it came free the silver lines fell back, faded for a moment and then brightened and shrank away through the floor.

'What are you going to do with it?'

'The river,' I replied without pausing in my stride. The main doorway was crackling with energy as I took the steps in a single leap and sped across the gravel towards the bridge.

It was too late, I knew that. What was left was no bigger than a marble, its energy drained off into the stonework of the college.

I was wheezing as I reached the bridge. It was that damned dust of course. It had permeated my body and I was sure it had, in some way, begun to direct my research.

As I hurled the meteor out into the rain-swollen current, the stone parapet was already pulsing with alien life. What reached the water was merely rock.

'Is that it?' asked The Dean, breathless, as he joined me on the bridge. But his answer was all around us. The college, the bridge, the dormitories, even the cottages lining the road approaching the university: all were pulsating with a fierce, cold light. The alien consciousness, life-force, sentience – call it what you would, was seeking out the stone and rock which provided the conditions which most suited its replication.

I explained my thoughts to The Dean as we watched the buildings light up in the distant village.

'It's a remote spot,' he said, hopelessly. 'Fifty miles

to the next town. Maybe it will find itself confined here and we can discover a way to bring it under control?'

I didn't give him an answer.

Along the valley, we could already see the lower flanks of the mountains beginning to coruscate against the darkening sky.

The ocean of sky

Time on their hands

So this, is likely where I die.

'ALlN, an inventory.'

>*Storage facility Rampton 771/AC1/55. 4m x 4m. Fully pressurized container unit. Current contents: One: Series 12, AI unit, Autonomous Laser Intelligence Networking installation. Two: portable packing-crate size 4. Empty. Three: 5 x bundles of 25mm x 5m hull insulation blanket. Four: Eighteen-hundred 50gm dehydrated provision pouches. Five: Andrew Card. Archivist, First Class, Gold Nugget, Gold Liner Services.*<

'And that's it?'

>*'Fraid so.*<

'Spare me the colloquialisms. I don't need a friendly room-mate right now. We're adrift in a jettisoned storage facility, light years from the nearest planetfall. What I need is a miracle, not a bio-engineered brain substitute.'

>*You said, "We"*<

'Sorry?'

>*You said, "We're adrift"; which suggests you already perceive me as a companion, of sorts.*<

'Of sorts. But you're right. I must guard against any form of anthropomorphism. Even a Series One can play tic tac toe. It doesn't make ALINs human my friend.'

The ocean of sky

>Friend?<

'You know what I mean. Now, use that legendary computing power to tell me, is there any way out of this situation?'

>Depends what you mean by "Out".<

'You're employing abbreviated syntax again. If it's a misguided attempt to introduce familiarity into our discourse and lower my stress levels - forget it. What do I mean by "Out"? I mean OUT, you box of synthetic neural-circuitry! As in "escape from", "get home", "return to the ship".'

>Escape from our current imprisonment would require a number of factors to fall into unlikely alignment.<

'Well, humour me ALIN. Enumerate, please.'

>This storage facility is not capable of independent flight. It is therefore on a trajectory determined by its initial random thrust at the time of the incident. I calculate that this trajectory will intercept a habitable system in approximately...<

'Approximately? What's with approximately? I thought you had a brain the size of a planet - figuratively speaking. Why can't I have accuracy?'

>Because the system referred to is some way off and I do not have data to support detailed analysis.<

'Some way off?'

>Approximately, fifty-three light years. Travelling at the speed of light that would take - <

'Fifty-three years, yeah, I get it. But we're not travelling at the speed of light, are we? What's your ETA for this hunk of steel?'

>One hundred and twenty-seven-thousand years

- give or take ten years either way.<

'Jeez! That's a mite too long to wait for planetary interception.'

>Actually, I determine that this container would intercept with that system's sun. A white dwarf which - <

'Never mind what kind of sun it is. It's not relevant. Where are those factors you spoke about earlier? The ones that need to come into alliance?'

>During the course of a one hundred and twenty-seven-thousand-year journey, there is an unquantifiable - <

'I like that word less than approximately.'

>My apologies but the chances to which I was about to allude cannot be calculated due to a lack of data. There is an unquantifiable possibility that this container will be tracked by an intelligent species and an equally unpredictable chance that said species will be able to investigate and thus effect rescue. Of course, it is likely that you will be long dead by the time of such an occurrence.<

'Too many unknowns. Give me something more positive.'

>The vessel which we left so hurriedly, will calculate our flight path, mobilise the nearest deep space vessel and, following at several times our own velocity, will overhaul us and make recovery.<

'Hey, I like that one a lot better. ls it a real possibility?'

>Given that our home vessel was destroyed by a cataclysmic explosion seconds after we were thrown free? No.<

The ocean of sky

'Destroyed? I didn't know that! How do you know that?'

>Because in the micro-second which elapsed after the meteor collision tore this container free from the external hold facility and before it rammed into the main superstructure of the Golden Nugget, I received communication via the ship's own Intelligence Network which made it clear that such a result was inevitable.<

'Glad to near that someone's sure about something! And so, there's no happy ending to this one then?'

>None at all I'm afraid.<

'You're learning.'

>Learning?<

'No, "'fraid not"! Shall we call it a day then?'

>Let's. Meteor Strike! Game One-hundred-and-fifty-two, terminated at 06.00 ship time.

>God, these deep space journeys are boring. What now Andy, fancy a game of tic tac toe?<

A life less colourful

Victor stepped down carefully from the doorway and surveyed the land around his new home. It lay pale and featureless beneath a sky filled with stars and for the first time in years, he felt truly at peace.

Wharf Street Estate had been drab and colourless. Walls of rain-stained concrete rising in perpendicular opposition to the flat, grey paving, tiled monotonously throughout its communal spaces. Where long dead architects had envisaged grass, a more resilient asphalt had been spread and beyond the underpass, the ring-road had run through monochromatic tower blocks to a putty-coloured river, flowing joylessly between hard granite banks.

From the fifteenth floor, Victor had been able to look out across the vast expanse of city and see no tones but those of stone and steel, save for the distant hills which showed as a dull, slate-blue smudge on the smoky horizon.

Childhood saw him playing among the drab walkways' concrete render and circling, on his bike, the car park's grubby, shadowed columns.

Later, the air-force took him into the desert, where the world was empty and mostly sky and what remained was merely a washed-out, ochre footnote, and it was there that he'd met Harper; red-haired,

The ocean of sky

green-eyed Harper.

He'd joined the programme by then and was well into initial training. She was the mission profiler, making assessments of psychological aptitude. In their sessions together he found himself wrong-footed time after time.

'Do you see yourself as a solitary sort of character, Victor?'

'Solitary? Do you mean, unsociable?'

'Do you prefer to use that description?'

'No. Certainly not. I don't think it's appropriate at all.'

'You prefer, solitary.'

'No, that's not what I meant...'

Sometimes he wasn't sure if she was following her professional brief or merely baiting him for the hell of it. One day, six weeks into the process, he'd asked her.

She'd grinned then, as if she'd been waiting for him to make the challenge.

'Can't it be both?'

'Can it?

'Maybe your answers are relevant to the programme and I'm prodding your butt for kicks.'

'Well, are you?'

'Just waitin' fer the invitation, cowboy!'

It had still taken him a long minute to register her response and decipher the content. Then he'd smiled back, tentatively. 'Consider the invitation extended,' he'd said, wonderingly.

She'd hit him hard, rolled him over and left him winded for the duration. By the time he'd taken breathe and taken stock, they were in Niagara and

A life less colourful

it wasn't until the third day, that they'd found time to take in The Falls.

'It's what you want, isn't it?' Six months had passed and both love and lust had run their course somewhat. The practical considerations of his work, which until now they had determinedly supressed, had become at length, a topic for debate.

'It's not a case of "want" Harper. I've put three years into the programme. I have responsibilities. A lot of people would be let down if I backed out now.'

'You know that's not true. There are half-a-dozen trainees in reserve; standing by in case of emergencies.'

'But it's not an emergency, is it? They've spent two-and-a-half million bucks on me already. Whaddya want me to say, "sorry chief, I met this girl..." ?'

'Oh, that's not fair, Vick! That's making it sound like I'm holding you back.'

'Well, aren't you?' The question was out before he considered the wisdom of voicing it.

She turned on him in anger. 'You see! It's just as I said. You don't see the problem as our shared relationship, you see it as one of us getting in the way of the other. Me, placing obstacles in the way of your ambition.'

He didn't know how to reply. The truth was that he was already weary of their new lifestyle. The round of social engagements; the new car; the house and its furnishings. The cursed kitchen with its black quartz worktops and contrasting orange cabinets.

The ocean of sky

The lounge and it's excruciating feature wall. Fuchsia Sunrise! or had they chosen the Cerise Miasma? He no longer cared – hadn't cared since they first moved in to their married quarters. There was something here he could not cope with. Maybe it was the painted walls and maybe it was Harper's fiery hair and emerald eyes. Or perhaps, it was her more expansive way of seeing the world. A dimension he had not learned to access.

'You should know,' he said, with only a little rancour, 'you're the expert. You're the one who spent two months drilling into my psyche and finding it wanting.'

She laughed, humourlessly. 'That's right. I should have known. After all, I identified your single-minded determination. It was one of the reasons I recommended you for the project. Bloody-minded obstinacy is another way of putting it.' She paused, as if unsure whether to proceed. 'That,' she said, carefully, 'and something else; something less tangible: a response mechanism that doesn't fire; a missing trigger that leaves you satisfied with less; enables you to function perfectly, in a world less…colourful.'

She paused and smiled at him sadly. 'Go, damn you. If I'm still here in five years' time, drop in and say hello.'

Victor stepped carefully down from the doorway and surveyed the land around his new home. The lunar regolith lay pale and grey beneath a black sky filled with stars and, as the Earth sank below the

Moon's near horizon and took with it the last trace of colour, he felt truly at peace for the first time in years.

The ocean of sky

To and fro

Halstead stood back and regarded, with considerable pride, the assembly of steel tubing and circuitry which together comprised the Temporal Phase Generator.

Now that it was at last complete, he felt an overwhelming sense of fulfilment; the culmination of three decades of research and development finally ready for field testing.

And there was a nervous anticipation too, he had to admit. Now that theory and calculation had transformed into the solid geometry of the device which stood before him; now that abstract concept had become concrete reality; this was the moment of truth, when he must put the tools of its construction behind him and climb on board; trust his life and well-being to the child of his creative imagination.

Seated at last within the field-containment structure, fingers poised above the screen's keyboard, he realised with mild amusement that he had previously given this moment no thought at all. It was thirty years since he had conceived a method by which it might be possible to travel through time; three decades during which he had devoted his whole life to realising that aim; but this was the first occasion on which he had been faced with consideration of just where to travel in all the aeons of existence; which year, relative to the present,

The ocean of sky

should he visit on this, his inaugural transit.

There were practical considerations of course. The very real possibility of rematerializing inside some later or earlier construction: a stone wall for instance, or a motorway flyover; or finding the ground levels to be significantly higher or lower. A better bet for a starting point would have been a natural rock formation - some place where things had been unchanged for centuries, other than by minor erosion; but finding such a spot and transporting all his equipment to it would be expensive and time-consuming. He realised with a smile that consuming time was the very least of his problems, although his diminishing budget was real enough.

Besides, he was impatient to be off.

There were other uncertainties about temporal transference. The maths took him from A to B but it did not resolve the paradoxes which were the bane of science fiction writers. He couldn't tell what would happen if he travelled to a time before his own existence; nor whether he could truly encounter himself and exist as two people living side by side. These were unknown and, possibly, unknowable.

He shrugged the thought aside. This was, after all, a field test and he would know the answers soon enough.

For the purpose of proving first principals there was no need to travel far; a year into the future would be enough, he thought. He had every expectation of still occupying this laboratory in ten years' time, which gave certainty of a safe arrival

To and fro

just twelve months hence. It would be the time too, when he would solve that 'dual existence' conundrum, because he fully intended to be waiting here for his own arrival! He doubted that the world would come to an end. More likely, he would see his other self as a ghost image with no chance of them interacting in any way.

Having made the decision, he set the coordinates for one year ahead, left the month, day and time as they stood in the present and touched the program button.

The transfer wasn't instantaneous. He hadn't expected it to be. For highly complex reasons he had predicted the time needed to be 30.64 seconds and so it proved to be: in validation of his theories.

During this half-minute or so, he experienced a disorientating blur of images while his view of the laboratory seemed to stretch to infinity and then suddenly snap back to normal at the moment the reading on-screen blinked forward to the next year.

He looked around. To his mild consternation the laboratory had altered significantly. Different equipment stood on the benches, cupboards had been moved, there were new blinds at the windows. Well, his research had ended with his first trial and so maybe it wasn't so unexpected that, during the ensuing year, he had made changes. The thing that worried him more was that there was no sign of his future self despite having had almost twelve months to prepare for the moment.

Was it possible that in the interim he had succumbed to a terminal illness? Been run over by the proverbial bus? That might account for the changes within the lab.

He frowned and examined the array. The year was correct, date and time just as when he had left. It was puzzling, no more. He'd make the return journey and examine the data. He tapped the keyboard to reverse the year to the one he had left and touched the button.

There was the same nauseating distortion of the scene around him, the same sudden return to normality.

He had time to check the reading - it was identical to the one at the outset of his journey - and then, as he noted this fact, the view distorted once more and 30.64 seconds later he was, again, in the newly arranged laboratory one year later.

He sat and considered the event. What circumstance had whipped him back for a second time? As he gave consideration to the matter the scene blurred and stretched and with a sharp clarity returned him to his starting point.

By the fourth occurrence he had it worked out. He didn't find himself in the future laboratory because he had not lived through the intervening year. He had merely travelled to and fro between the same two points in time, always arriving just before the moment of departure. There was no paradox. When he travelled forward in time, he reached the exact microsecond at which he set off for home; and when he reached home, it was at the precise moment that he set off into the future.

He had fixed himself on a loop of existence from which there was no escape. He had become an immortal with only one minute to live

Captive audience

'It doesn't make sense,' said Commander Josh McKenzie, for the dozenth time that morning. 'None at all.'

Ensign Larry Chivers, who had been leaning on the door frame and staring into the strange environment beyond the thick glass observation window, rolled his eyes towards the heavens and swore silently; then he turned and addressed his senior officer.

'With respect sir, there's really no reason why it should: they're aliens, sir.'

'Of course they're aliens!' growled the Commander, 'we didn't come halfway across the galaxy to visit our in-laws. Naturally their behaviour is going to be different to our own, predicated on their own evolutionary and historical development but, even so, you'd expect certain inevitable responses to a given situation.'

'But why sir?'

'Because they're clearly a highly intelligent race of beings with a sophisticated technology. That suggests enquiring minds, a desire to investigate and learn from their experiences...' he paused, let his shoulders slump in exasperation and waved his hands despairingly towards the glass. 'Instead, they seem to accept captivity as the end of the matter; as if life in a zoo was about the best anyone could hope for. Damn it! Why won't they communicate with us? Why this dumb acceptance of the role of... exhibits! They must see that there's so much more

The ocean of sky

to be gained from species interaction.'

'It's not as if we were aggressive or anything,' mused the Ensign. 'We went through all the protocols for establishing friendly relations with alien beings. If they hadn't reacted the way they did, there wouldn't have been any need to lock anyone up.'

'Exactly! So, what sparked them off in the first place? It's illogical.'

The ensign, a fan of early 2D sci-fi, grinned involuntarily as an image of the commander with pointed ears flashed across his mind.

'Maybe you see this situation as amusing, Chivers?'

'No sir! Well, that is sir, there is a certain humour in the situation, sir, don't you think...sir?' His voice trailed off apprehensively as the unlikelihood of the commander finding anything to laugh about in their current predicament became immediately obvious.

'Hrrmph.' The commander chose not to respond further and instead, took the ensign's place at the door and made his own observation of the steamy exterior.

The inhabitants of the planet which the ship's data banks had unimaginatively designated as Quadrant Seven, 2003-147-779, were unprepossessing creatures. They were grey, shaggy, humanoids with a number of appendages, the purposes of which, in most cases, remained unclear. A few of them were out there now, checking equipment, monitoring, he assumed, conditions on the other side of the door. Attempts to attract their attention had proved fruitless: it seemed obvious that the crew's waving

Captive audience

and shouting must have been noted by the aliens but up until now there had been a singular lack of response.

What were they expecting of their human visitors? Were they indeed expecting anything? What the hell was going on in their inscrutable little alien minds? The Commander made to kick at the door, realised the futility of such an action and lowered his foot to the floor with deliberate self-control.

When the ISA Grand Alliance had first made contact with the entities known for the time being as 'Quads', response had been minimal but positive, none-the-less. The planet's inhabitants were technologically competent and just beginning the exploration of their own system with robotic probes. Even so, receiving sudden and unexpected communication from a race of space-faring humans must have been a challenging moment and it was to be expected that they would proceed with caution when considering their visitors' offers of friendship. But, as the Ensign had noted, all appropriate protocols had been observed and there had been every reason to expect a cordial, if wary, exchange of views at the first face to face meeting between the two species.

So, when the Quads had retreated through their airlock and left the party from Earth alone in the balanced, Earth-normal environment of the meeting chamber, the Commander had assumed the move was the precursor to some sort of welcoming ceremony: the moment when the walls drew apart and the President of Quadrant Seven – or some such dignitary – strode in and offered the

The ocean of sky

hand of peace and brotherhood to the people of Earth. The Commander grimaced. That was how it worked in the movies and, damn it, he'd been rather looking forward to playing his part in a moment of history.

Except that the President hadn't appeared and nor had any other representative of the Quad civilisation. The group chosen to make up the Earth's welcoming committee had waited, at first patiently and then with increasing levels of frustration and concern until they had at last come to understand that they were not revered guests but simple captives.

That was when they tried beating on the walls and signalling to the aliens through the glass door panel. To no effect whatsoever.

They'd made contact with their own ship easily enough and explained their predicament. The ship had tried raising the Quads to find out what was going on but had received no reply. With no dialogue taking pace, threats of repercussions if the humans were not released lacked weight and anyway, the ship was only lightly armed and any sort of back-up was five light years distant.

It simply wasn't a scenario which the writers of the Extra-terrestrial Contact Procedures Program had foreseen. Aggression, yes. Fear, certainly. The possibility of superior intellect and religious mania had both been given due consideration. But the idea that the newly discovered race might accept initial advances before locking you up and losing interest...no.

That had been two days ago; now things were

Captive audience

beginning to get serious.

To begin with, they had been supplied with no food. Their environment suits contained enough nutrients to sustain life for a week and the recyclers might keep them going for two but that was stretching it.

And then there was the air supply; if there was an air supply. The hall was large and it was too soon to judge the effects of carbon dioxide toxicity or oxygen deprivation but if the Quads were as indifferent to their charges as seemed apparent, then they were all living on borrowed time.

They might, Commander McKenzie was forced to accept, die here in this empty room, on this distant planet, and no-one would be any the wiser as to what it was all about.

Frustration and despair had just about reached their nadir when he looked up and saw that for the first time since their incarceration, one of the aliens beyond the door seemed to be paying them some attention.

He, she - who could define the gender of the hirsute creatures? – was looking back over its shoulder in what he fancied might be a surreptitious manner, whilst ostensibly checking the display on a piece of wall-mounted equipment.

Seeing him watching, the Quad turned quickly away, hunched its frame and began to shake gently.

What curious piece of behaviour was this? thought the Commander as the creature suddenly fell to its pseudo-knees whilst supporting itself on a pair of forward limbs.

By now, another Quad had noticed its fellow's

The ocean of sky

conduct and had come across to investigate. It crouched enquiringly, tipped its own head in seeming acknowledgement and then began the same shaking. All at once a crowd of the hairy beings appeared and began slapping each other's backs, resting their forelimbs on their knees and indulging in the same curious juddering activity.

The door between the Commander and the aliens was soundproof but, even without an accompanying sound-track, an understanding began to slowly dawn on him.

'The sons of...!' he roared, bringing ensign Chivers running to his side.

'Yes sir? What is it sir? Hey! The Quads are doing something! Er, what *are* they doing, sir?'

The Commander turned his fiercest countenance on his subordinate. Not for nothing was he known as "old thunderhead" to ranks below decks.

'I realise, Mr Chivers, that attributing human characteristics to extra-terrestrials is a fraught business but, if I'm reading them aright,' he glowered out to where some of the Quads were now holding their sides and pointing in the humans' direction, 'those Goddamned, long-haired reprobates are LAUGHING at us!'

'Did the dinner go well, sir?'

Chief Petty Officer Patterson removed his cap, placed it carefully under his arm and fell into step with his Commanding Officer. Given what had gone before, he awaited the answer to his enquiry with a degree of apprehension.

In his view, the old man had shown considerable

restraint and diplomacy when finally acquainted with the cultural traditions of their new friends.

'The dinner? Oh, that went well enough,' they had reached the Commander's quarters and the senior officer entered, beckoning for his subordinate to follow, 'given that neither guests nor hosts were able to eat each other's food and all conversation went, by necessity, via the ship's AI.' He paused in his narrative to nod agreement to the Chief's silent enquiry concerning a drink and continued, 'so yes, our actual dinner was first class, as usual - convey my complements to everyone in the galley, will you?'

Patterson poured a generous measure of Scotch and passed it to the Commander. He'd noted the emphasis given to the satisfactory nature of that one particular element of the evening's entertainment and assumed that there was another, perhaps more interesting, yet to be revealed. He probed gently.

'Any further discussion about the little reception party they threw when we touched down?'

The Commander moved the whisky thoughtfully around his palate. Once released from temporary captivity, he had received the initial explanation of the Quad's behaviour from Chian, the ship's astrobiologist, and, after counting to ten, had felt it prudent to leave further investigation of the aliens' cultural mores to the specialist.

In the event, Chian's later report simply confirmed his original supposition: that the whole meet and greet had been an elaborate charade designed to cause maximum embarrassment to the visiting Earthmen.

The ocean of sky

'The Broonty – that's their own name for their race - have a creator-myth concerning the god, Vantarontal. He was a prankster who brought their world into being as an amusement for his fellow deities. A sort of cosmic-scale parlour trick. The Broonty no longer believe in such tales of course but the idea of comedic enterprise runs deep in their psyche. A hoax, like the one played on your welcoming committee, is the highest form of compliment that they can pay. Really sir, you should feel flattered.'

Reports of his response to this suggestion, had by now he reflected, probably become part of the ship's own folklore.

He swallowed, felt the satisfaction of the spirit burning into his gut and looked up.

'Yes, we were the butt of a bit more finger pointing and juvenile giggling,' he said, as the Chief filled his own glass and took a proffered chair. 'I have to admit I've found the whole matter of their imbedded tradition bloody difficult to take on board. Still, I thought we'd handled ourselves quite well; maintained the correct degree of diplomatic sangfroid. Up until their latest stunt, that is.'

The Chief widened his eyes, suddenly all attention.

'We'd just got to the part of the proceedings where, had we been at home, it would have been time for the speeches. On cue, the senior honcho climbs to his furry feet. Grand Superior is the nearest the AI can come to a title which acquaints to our own epithets. So, there he stands - shaggy-coated, features almost hidden by that long, straggle of hair, and with those seemingly redundant appendages that no one has ever seen them use...'

'Yes?' interjected the Chief, his impatience overcoming his discretion.

'When,' the Commander rose to his feet to better illustrate what he was about to describe, 'he reaches up under his chin and...' Commander McKenzie raised his hand to the knot of his tie and ran it deftly, finger and thumb clenched, from neckline to crotch, ' - he unzips the whole fucking outfit!'

For a while Chief Petty Officer Patterson was too stunned to speak. When at last he found he could manage a breathless response, he asked, 'What did you do, sir? I mean, what could you do?'

McKenzie stood, still in the act of tugging on an imaginary zip-fastener and slowly, a grin spread across his swarthy countenance.

'What did I do, Chief? What did I do? I laughed my bloody head off, that's what I did! And everybody else joined in – AND,' he roared the conjunction in triumph – 'the declaration of Human/Broonty Concord was signed and sealed the same evening!'

The Chief couldn't help grinning too. The vision of his Commanding Officer faced with such a circumstance was worthy of the Broonty's own acclamation.

'Well done, sir! I must say, you showed presence of mind in your reaction. I'm pretty sure I'd have just stared, gobsmacked.'

'Ah,' the Commander placed a hand on his Chief Petty officer's shoulder and regarded him with the trace of a smile, 'but then, you didn't see what the Grand Superior had *under* his suit!'

The ocean of sky

The last Martian

I watched them arrive, the Earthmen. A crack opened in the sky and their descent sealed it closed again. A tight, white light that scoured the rocks as it shrank down, until their craft was swallowed in the billowing red dust.

When the dust had settled, they climbed down and made the long walk to my home. I sat by the door and waited to give them entry.

The first to reach me raised a hand and spoke. The sound of his words was strange but I knew their meaning.

He said, 'Greetings old man, we come at last, to reunite our two worlds.'

It seemed to me that he had practised this speech - but what do I know of conversation? I stood and offered my hand, as my father had taught me in preparation for this moment.

'One day,' he had said, 'they will return. They did not do so in my father's time - though he thought they might – but the day will come.'

'Yes,' I had replied, 'but will I still live when they do come, these mysterious Earthmen?'

He had not answered my question.

Now, the visitor took my hand and grasped it firmly. 'Where are the others?' he asked and he frowned a little as he looked around.

The ocean of sky

'There are no others,' I told him, and it was the first time I had spoken since my father died. 'My mother did not survive my birth. I remember a little of my grandfather. My father said that once there were many but their numbers dwindled.'

'There were several hundred when the colony was formed,' said the second visitor, whose voice was lighter and whose features were softer than the other, 'but that was a century and a half ago.'

'The settlement, where is the settlement?' said the first, turning a full circle as he scanned the terrain.

'Under the dunes,' I said, '– or so my father told me. 'It was abandoned after the outbreak.'

That caught their attention. 'What outbreak?' they chorused.

'Some illness,' I said. 'It was long ago; I know a little about it. Father said that people became sick and died. It was soon after their arrival. The scientists among them worked hard to find a cure but it came too late. He said that things would have been different if Earth had not forgotten them.'

'We didn't forget!' The smaller visitor, who I wondered might be a woman, spoke up insistently. 'The pandemic of which you heard? It swept the Earth too. Billions died there. Society collapsed. It has taken decades to rebuild, to regain our ability to travel between the planets. We had hoped that you would be free from the contagion; free to thrive and expand. But the infection must already have been with you, brought by the first colonists.'

'No,' I interrupted. 'You carried it back. It originated here. Some result of the work done to make this part

The last Martian

of the planet habitable. So my father said.'

'The paraterraforming programme? But that was carried out hundreds of years ago, utilising the local cave systems. They enlarged them and sealed them under a pressurised roof. The hope was that as your population grew you would expand the colony in the same way. As it is, it's a wonder that the integrity of the system has been maintained for so long - the oxygenation and deep-water extraction.'

'Oh, there have been crises in the past and I only make use of a fraction of the original space. Any system failure now will likely kill me. Meanwhile, I go on growing my own food and there are still stores enough for hundreds. I manage.'

The woman shook her head inside the transparent bubble of her helmet. 'How ironic. We thought at one time that you might be the only hope for the future of mankind; that the race would survive here even if disease decimated the Earth. And all along you were the source of the disaster.' She laughed, mirthlessly.

'Well,' said her companion, 'the great adventure is over. One day we may try again to establish ourselves on this planet but now it's time for you to return home, old man.'

'Return? Home?' I looked scornfully at my two "rescuers". 'How can I make a return to a planet on which I have never set foot? How can you call Earth my home when I was born and have lived my whole life in this very dome? I have no wish to accompany you on your journey back. This is my home and here I shall stay; I am content to be the last Martian.

The ocean of sky

Mind games

It wasn't until Stephanie was lying back on the pillow and waiting for sleep to enfold her, that the surreal nature of the whole undertaking suddenly became apparent and, as Adrian bent over and ran his fingers through her hair, her lips formed into an involuntary smile.

He was weird, on that point everyone at uni was in agreement: lacking social graces, he had few friends and little inclination to make new ones. Fellow students in the science faculty found him difficult to work with and shunned his company, although they admitted grudgingly to a sharp intellect and single-minded dedication; but in general, the student body found him odd and so, had any of them been aware, they would have considered it more than surprising when Stephanie accepted an invitation to spend a night in his bed.

'Do you know anything about astral projection?'

The question was so incongruous that for a moment Stephanie had no answer available. She had known Adrian since early childhood and had learned to steer her way around his peculiarly direct forms of address and careless rudeness; but she knew he was dedicated to scientific investigation and the idea that he might have any interest in mysticism or such exotic practices as mind travel

The ocean of sky

was extraordinary.

'You mean, out-of-body experiences?' she said at last, studying his face for some emotional indicator. He wouldn't be making a joke - Adrian didn't do humour – and he didn't drink either, so inebriation wasn't a factor.

'Yes, the idea that your consciousness can move, independent of the physical form. You've heard of the phenomena?'

'Well, yes but you don't believe in that mumbo-jumbo surely, Adrian?'

'I think it might be possible, yes. I believe the practice may have been misunderstood in the past. You've heard of the multiple-universe theory? The idea that existence may be divided into infinite layers of reality?'

'Er, yes, it's something to do with quantum science isn't it?'

Stephany still felt wrong-footed. When Adrian had unexpectedly asked her to join him in his lab one evening, she had not known what to expect from the encounter. It would be no amorous tryst of that she was confident. If Adrian had sexual predilections, he had never revealed them to her and there was nothing suggestive of a chat-up line as he conducted her around the equipment and halted before a cage of large, white rats.

'Quantum scientists have propounded the theory, yes, and their findings tie-in with my own investigations into brain function in a rather unexpected manner.

'During sleep there are two quite distinct periods, of which REM-sleep is the most studied. REM stands for...'

'Rapid eye movement,' Stephanie interrupted, keen to show some basic knowledge of the subject under discussion.

'That's right, it follows a longer period of deep sleep, which is where my interest lies.' He indicated the rats, who, in expectation perhaps of a meal, had crowded to the front of their enclosure and raised themselves on their back legs, forepaws grasping the metal bars. 'Experiments with these rodents suggest that something much more fundamental is occurring during that period. I believe, Stephany, that during deep sleep, the consciousness really does migrate, although it doesn't, in my opinion leave the body, as such.'

'I don't follow.' And really, there was no reason why she should, thought Stephany, offering up a finger for one of the larger rats to nuzzle.

'I am almost sure that when the mind gives-up control of the body to autonomous functions and plunges into deep sleep, that in fact it slips from this plain of existence into another: a parallel world where, for a time, it occupies an alternate mind in an alternate version of the self.'

'But why? What's the point?' If this was science it was more bizarre than the mysticism she had earlier derided.

'At this stage, who can tell? Remember, the other existence is not some distant world; it overlaps our own, maybe even merges with it. The transition may be to a state of complete rest or maybe to offer some assistance to that other self. We may have evolved as multiple-world beings. A duplicate

The ocean of sky

existence may be necessary to our well-being. Perhaps, without knowing it, we have always been creatures of merged identity; each layer interacting with the others in some mysterious meld.'

'So why do you want me?' asked Stephany, puzzled but intrigued by the vision of such a being.

'I can only discover so much with rats,' replied Adrian, 'I need a human to follow through with what I have already learned. It will be entirely non-invasive: just some electrodes to study brain patterns during deep sleep – and a couple of other devices to trigger separation.'

'Hang on, what are "a couple of other devices" exactly?'

'When you are at a certain low point in neural activity the sensors will cut in and fire a low-power pulse to stimulate disengagement from one consciousness to another. I will simply record the results and you will sleep on to the REM phase and wake in due course.'

'And is there an element of danger in all this?' asked Stephany, suspiciously.

Adrian looked back blankly, as if he had not understood the question.

And so, here she was; drifting off to sleep as Adrian adjusted the electrodes amongst her hair. She'd not felt able to refuse. They had been friends since childhood and she was probably the only person who understood his fractured personality, now that his mother was dead. She'd had a night on the town with the girls, to make herself properly tired and then left them without telling of her plans for the rest of the night.

She soothed her slight concerns with the knowledge that her dysfunctional friend was most probably a genius and she might one day have a footnote in his citation for a Nobel Prize. It was her last thought as she sank away into oblivion.

She woke, muzzy-headed and uncomfortable; she seemed to have lain awkwardly, her body hard against the wall next to the bed. She stretched and, with difficulty, climbed to her feet; her limbs seemed uncoordinated and cramped. Blinking the sleep from her eyes she reached up, grasped for a handhold and peered out into the laboratory.

She screamed as soon as her whiskers encountered the bars of the cage.

The ocean of sky

Right and wrong

'I know it's not for me to question the world leader in the new technology sir, but don't you think that there's something a little unnatural about that ear sir?'

'Keep an eye on that arterial pressure Mr Carter, I don't want it to drop below 70. Unnatural you say? Well, I know that some people see 3D printing of body parts as a little unnerving. A touch of the Mary Shelley's as it were. But I would have thought that as a man of science Mr Carter, you would have seen beyond such foolishness.'

'I do sir, I assure you. What I meant was – well, it doesn't look quite right somehow.
Er, NBP is one-hundred over sixty. Diastoloc 75.'

'This ear, young man, was grown in the lab on a printed scaffold of hydrogel alginate, seeded with the patient's own cells. It is almost indistinguishable from the patient's other ear, which was scanned and copied into a computer program and that is why it's such an extraordinarily good match. To all intents and purposes, it is the same ear. Every fold and texture duplicated to the finest detail. If you were to stand the two side by side, so to speak, I don't think you'd be able to tell me which was the original and which the copy.'

'Isn't that the point sir? I mean, shouldn't it be just a bit different sir? In nature the two would have

The ocean of sky

particular characteristics which would distinguish them, one from the other.'

'What, you mean a freckle – or a mole maybe? Mmm, it's a thought for the future Carter. A spot of artistic individualism perhaps. Yes, I like that, it's something to ponder, after the operation.'

'That wasn't quite what I was getting at sir. It's this particular ear that's troubling me.'

'Look Carter, the construction of this ear was overseen by me at every step in the process. It is as lifelike as any medical prosthesis could possibly be. It is the product of the most advanced procedures currently available. What more than absolute conformity to its partner ear could you possibly demand?'

'Well sir, it's just that...should they both be right ears sir? Shouldn't the new one be just a bit, leftish?'

Bad timing

'Look, the thing I'm trying to make you understand is that I've travelled through time. I'm not of your world. I'm a scientist, that's the point. I deal with concepts you would simply not comprehend.'

Halstead tried to make a gesture which would indicate his frustration but the shackles bit into his wrists as the chains arrested the movement and he squealed in discomfort.

'Isn't it obvious?' he insisted, determined to make his point. 'You only have to look at my equipment to see that it's far beyond your own primitive technology.' This time, as he pointed towards the temporal displacement generator, the wrought iron band pulled tight again and drew blood.

He gritted his teeth against the pain and forced himself to examine the room in more detail.

It was small, square, brick-built and windowless. The only light came from the fire which burned behind a lattice of stout, metal bars and above which, a wide, black, metal funnel drew smoke into an unseen chimney. Near the fire was a table made of thick, wooden beams, its edges worn and, in places, charred black like the fire-hood. On its top were an assortment of tongs and pokers, and odd devices which Halstead could not identify, with screw-threads and greased gears.

He looked back at the only other person in the

The ocean of sky

room, a tall, angular man with a full-sleeved shirt, some kind of elaborate waistcoat and knee-length breeches. He was regarding Halstead not with hostility but with an intelligent curiosity, which Halstead hoped might offer an opportunity for sensible dialogue, despite the shackles.

'So,' said the other, speaking for the first time since he had entered and waved dismissal to the grubby miscreant who had chained Halstead to the wall, 'you confess to your arrival from the nether world? Good, we may bring an end to this interview before nightfall. Come then, since you are eager to unburden yourself, tell me your purpose here. What is it your evil master demands of you? Do you act for Spain in this matter?'

The questions were civilly enough put but their content was disappointing thought Halstead. They didn't suggest the enlightened world-view for which he had hoped.

'I don't have a master, evil or otherwise,' he replied, trying to keep his voice light and unconcerned, 'unless you mean the Dean of course! He can be pretty intimidating I admit.'

He forced a laugh but it came out more like a wheeze. Damn it! He just had to turn up here, didn't he? He'd known it was unwise to set off from the oldest part of college but his concerns then had been rematerializing within some ancient wall or finding the ground level to be several feet higher or lower. Somewhere on a natural rock outcrop where erosion had been minimal would have been ideal but when Penshurst had tipped him off about the Dean's imminent visit and he'd foreseen the

Bad timing

withdrawal of his research grant, there was no time to move the TDG to a more sensible location. He'd pulled on the harness and fired the generator and... the next thing he knew he was being roughly hauled from the device and chained-up.

He had complete faith in his invention and so he had quickly accepted that he was in an earlier century but which it was, his meagre understanding of history was unable to reveal. Sometime in the 16th was his guess. What little he had heard of the language had utilised odd vowel sounds and a few words which meant nothing to him but in general he was having no great difficulty in understanding or being understood; and despite the blood at his wrists he felt in no imminent danger.

He was confident that, despite the suggestive nature of the implements on the table, once he could engage in a rational dialogue with his interrogator, a common sense of intellectual integrity could be established and suspicion turned to fascination and a sharing of the scientific imperative, which he himself found so compelling.

That was when the man swung his arm back and struck Halstead hard across the mouth with the back of his gloved hand.

The blow split his lip and spattered blood across his face.

'For Christ's sake!' exclaimed Halstead, when he had regained enough of his senses to protest. 'There's no need for brutality. I'm not planning to be uncooperative. Look, with the secret of that device over there, you could become the most powerful man in history. Just unchain me and I'll

The ocean of sky

show you how it works.'

The man looked at him narrowly. 'And surely, you are the devil's spawn. For every word confirms your mission amongst us! You invoke our saviour's name and make the same promise which Satan made to Him in the wilderness. For he said, "All these things will I give thee, if thou wilt fall down and worship me." '

Halstead shook his head vigorously. 'I don't want your veneration, man, I'm just asking you to release me, so that I can explain how my device works. I'm an inventor, not a messenger from hell! Or Spain, for that matter. I make things - clever things if you will – but still just machines in their way; harnessing the forces of nature, not calling on occult powers!'

His antagonist snorted. ' 'Twould be a clever machine indeed that could carry a man from one day to another; a novel arrangement of cogs and springs, to unwind time and move its pointer from yesteryear to the morrow. Me thinks it would require a cunning clockmaker to becomes master of the temporal realm.'

'And yet,' said Halstead grabbing at the opportunity to take the dialogue into more familiar territory, 'I am such a man - and that device,' he nodded towards the generator, which leaned awkwardly against the further wall, 'is just such an instrument. With it you really can move backwards and forwards through time. Without,' he added hastily, 'any recourse to supernatural powers. Let me show you.'

The man chose to ignore his request but turned

Bad timing

and approached the TDG cautiously, prodding at part of its harness with one foot. 'How does it move?' he asked at length, having studied the box-shaped outlines and irregular surface details. 'I see no wheels. Perhaps you fly?'

The question was either derisive or intended to illicit an admission of necromancy but Halstead decided to treat it as a genuine request for enlightenment.

'It doesn't move as such,' he began hesitantly, aware that he needed to make his explanation as comprehensible as possible, allowing for his listener's limited understanding. 'It distorts the world around it to find a different place in the continuum. That is,' he hurried on, 'another point along the ribbon of space and time.'

That was rubbish of course. Mere technobabble designed to impress first year students and likely to elicit only scorn or violence from his interrogator. He tensed in expectation of at least a verbal assault but the other seemed to have become intrigued by the device's appearance. After a few moments of experimentation, he thrust his arms into the webbing and closed the fixing with a snap.

'Is this the way of the thing?' he asked and, for the first time Halstead heard intrigue rather than suspicion in his voice.

'Yes, that's right,' he nodded, 'the straps are just to ensure a close contact with the generator. 'Now try touching the small, square panel near your right hand.'

Halstead licked the blood from his lip. This was encouraging. If he could just engage the man's

The ocean of sky

interest, maybe they could, after all, establish some kind of scientific rapport. He tensed as the control screen came to life, displaying the co-ordinates and programming-keys but the reaction of his captor was more of fascination than fear. After only a brief hesitation he reached out and wonderingly, ran his fingers over the glowing surface.

It was only then that Halstead felt a moment of disquiet; a micro-second before the man and the temporal displacement generator blinked out of existence.

The Dean squared his shoulders and marched, resolutely, into the laboratory. He was not fond of confrontations of this sort. There would be wailing and a gnashing of teeth that was for sure but in difficult times like these, savings he supposed, must be achieved, cuts must be made. Ill-defined research projects like those undertaken in this facility, whilst admirable in their intent, were seen as unlikely to deliver a return anytime soon on the not inconsiderable sums invested. And fiscal integrity was, the Vice Chancellor had assured him, in a trying meeting only that afternoon, 'absolutely and entirely, the name of the game.'

The Dean had not met the Head of Temporal Studies personally, the department having been set up by his predecessor, and circumstances since had conspired to keep the incumbent and himself apart. It was for that reason that he had felt it more diplomatic to come to the laboratory rather than summon the man to his office to tell him the bad news.

Bad timing

Never the less, despite their lack of contact, he was aware that Professor Halstead was something of an eccentric and so, he was not unduly surprised by the outré appearance of the figure whom he discovered disengaging himself from a harness, attached to a strange, angular construction adorned with lights and buttons.

'Ah, Professor Halstead,' began the Dean, 'I am sorry to interrupt your important work,' and then, acknowledging that he was about to announce matters which would do rather more than "interrupt" proceedings, he added quickly, 'I wonder if I might have a word with you on a particularly delicate issue?'

The man the Dean supposed to be the professor, lowered the equipment to the ground and turned a wide-eyed and suspicious gaze on his visitor.

'Tell me, sir, whom you might be and what this place.'

The Dean was taken aback by both the style and the nature of the question but chose to deal with the part which made immediate sense. 'We have not met, Professor, and I must offer you my apologies for that. I am the recently appointed Dean.' He held out a hand which the other man chose to ignore. 'Do you think we might go to your office? I'm afraid that I have some unfortunate news to impart.'

The man regarded him shrewdly. 'You were mentioned to me sir. I am told you have an intimidating nature.'

The Dean raised his eyebrows. 'I think maybe that too is a reference to the one who went before.' He frowned, aware that he was already mimicking the

The ocean of sky

other man's oddly formal speech patterns.

'Please,' he placed a hand on the man's shoulder and guided him towards a glass-fronted cubicle which stood towards one side of the room. Inside, he waved to a chair and sat himself opposite.

'I won't beat about the bush Professor, there has been a review of college funding and this department is one of the unfortunate...victims.' Damn, that wasn't a word he'd have chosen with more time for consideration.

The "professor" meanwhile, had taken possession of the desk and now sat, hands steepled, a look of mild amusement on his face.

'The world,' he said, 'goes ever about its business,' and when the Dean looked puzzled by the remark, he waved it away and continued, 'I assume you know of the prodigious advances made herein?' and he gestured again, this time to indicate the surrounding building. 'I can but vouchsafe my own good offices in regard it.'

The Dean looked back uncomfortably. He should have dealt with this situation long ago; but there had been so many other things with which to get up to speed and no one had suggested that things had got this bad. Halstead was obviously deranged: the baggy shirt, the waistcoat - the knee-breeches for God's sake! And this Oldee English language! Something had tipped him over the edge and telling him his research grant had been removed was only going to make matters much worse. Still, there was no going back now.

'It's regrettable, of course it is and I know how much time and energy and...sheer bloody dedication you must have put into your work here but the die is cast, there's no turning the clock back and...' he found he'd run out of suitable metaphors and ended lamely, 'you'll need to be out by the end of October.'

He'd found it difficult to look the professor in the eye during this final statement and when he did return his gaze to the desk, he found it empty.

Almost simultaneously he felt something cold and sharp-edged at his throat and heard a voice whisper with a chilling, controlled malice into his ear.

Professor Nigel Halstead sat back in his chair and surveyed the busy scene beyond his office window. The extra students had made an incredible difference to the productivity of the department. Doubling the budget had moved things on by leaps and bounds – as any halfway intelligent person would have seen it would – and a couple of months would see them ready to launch their new, spin-off technology on world markets.

The time travel – well, that was being kept under wraps, by order of the Home Office. He'd sworn the official secrets act, as had Sir Francis – in his case a rather curious undertaking since the legislation in question had not been enacted until three-hundred years after his death – and only the PM knew if and how it might ever be used for the benefit of the nation and the world in general.

The PM and perhaps, Sir Francis Walsingham.

Halstead had a suspicion that there were meetings more covert than those that he was allowed to attend and that maybe, subtle interventions in the

The ocean of sky

temporal flux had already been made.

Any alterations such adjustments brought about, further down the time-line, would of course be unfathomable even to Hasltead. Changes in Sixteenth Century England would alter future events and render them normal to those who lived after. His own life might already have seen its path amended and he might no longer be the person he had been before - although he knew that was an illogical thought; there was no "before", the past was the past: if the clock had been reset then time had unfolded again for the very first time and could be made to do so over and over again.

He was unsure that he approved of such meddling. What history might Walsingham persuade them to rewrite? He was a man of formidable intellect and his influence would be extensive in both his own and the present century.

Halstead, weak on history, had read up on Philippian England and on the Spanish occupation of the intervening centuries and he was aware of Walsingham's antipathy towards the present Spanish king. The new left-wing government had its own agenda with regard to the monarchy and who could say how things would pan out?

Halstead sighed and logged off his PC. Agricultural research was a fascinating area of activity but he sometimes wondered if he might have followed a different path. He'd read Wells as a child and harboured fantasies of manipulating time. Later he'd flirted with quantum mechanics but had drifted into other fields of research. You never knew where you'd end up. It was a funny old world.

Nuisance call

It had been Jancethrip's conceit to bring the star vessel into orbit on manual, guiding it through the small system of planets by text-book navigation; but his pretensions didn't run as far as parking it in orbit and he waited patiently while the ship-brain nudged his craft into a thrix-perfect position which it would hold by constant vigilance and occasional burns of the thruster array.

Having been appraised of the success of this undertaking by a soft chime from the console, he reached out a limb and activated the communications sensor.

He had chosen his intercept carefully - there had been plenty of time to do so, his journey having taken the equivalent of four-hundred solar orbits by the planet currently under observation – and he was, therefore, surprised and a little annoyed when, no sooner had he brought the channel into life, than a voice filled the comfortable confines of his cabin.

He had rehearsed his introduction to the people of Earth a hundred times and refined it with each new performance and he was a little irked that it should be they who began the conversation and not him.

'Hello?' said the voice and, in the event, the word spoken seemed to represent merely the simplest of basic greetings with an inflection which appeared to invite a response.

'Greetings!' replied Jancethrip, utilising what was,

he had learned from monitoring the planet's airwaves, a positive and friendly tone. 'I come in peace to...'

'Am I speaking to the householder?' interrupted the voice, and Jancethrip's personal data implant registered an ingratiating tone whilst at the same time supplying information on the context of the question.

"Householder" – one responsible for the place in which they reside.

For a moment he was taken aback by the unexpected questioning of his status.

His implant, sensing his discomposure, offered clarification.

It may be merely a request for confirmation that you are the person in authority onboard this ship. My research suggests that, among this race the preferred form of address when encountering a new species is, "take me to your leader". The speaker may simply be seeking assurance that you hold that position.

Jancethrip groaned, inwardly. He'd hardly utterer a word and already the conversation was open to ambiguity and misunderstanding. It was difficult enough coping with the patterns and colloquialisms of a single language, but on this planet, they spoke a different tongue on opposite sides of the same hill!

Of course, he could leave the whole thing to the ship-brain; it would have analysed the subject, in depth, on the long journey from home, and no doubt it was familiar with every form of articulation in existence on the blue-green world spinning slowly below their craft. It could probably ask the

Nuisance call

time of day from a passing groveshatter – if they had such creatures down there but, Jancethrip told himself with a growl, Tharn would freeze over before he handed a species contact over to an artificial!

He sat up straight and flexed his upper arms in a determined manner.

'I am that personage.' he replied with what he hoped was an intonation suggestive of seniority.

'Good morning,' said the voice, 'Were you aware that the government has in place a scheme to compensate householders for the expense of upgrading their domestic heating facility?'

As Jancethrip's implant struggled to decipher the full context of this information, the voice continued, hurriedly, 'There is, available now, a scrappage scheme which can be worth up to three-hundred pounds if we were commissioned to replace your existing boiler.'

Their government appears to have a plan to reward you for the expenditure of time and effort in visiting their planet, the implant whispered inside his head. *A medal, perhaps? Some kind of certificate? Anyway, they are concerned at the condition of your life-support system. After that the language becomes technical and I cannot offer an accurate translation, but I sense that they are ready to send a supply rocket with replacement parts.*

But that's nonsense! replied Jancethrip, silently. Their technology is generations behind ours. Do they even have the capability to send up that much equipment?

The ocean of sky

They mention a load capacity of three-hundred pounds, which I calculate is roughly equivalent to double your own body-weight.

'Hello Sir? Are you still there?'

'Yes, yes, I'm here,' said Jancethrip, 'look, I don't need an upgrade, thank you. My current set-up is working at maximum efficiency. Your offer is most kind but could I reiterate that I come in peace as an ambassador of the...'

'May I ask how old your boiler is, sir? As time passes an unavoidable loss of efficiency soon costs you money. The government's scheme could save you thousands of pounds over several years of operation.'

'Huh, how old...?' stuttered Jancethrip. 'Well, I don't think I know.' How old is the damn LSS? He demanded of his implant.

Sixteen pathlans, give or take an ortix or two, instructed the implant. *I think they are referencing an old Earth maxim, a stitch in time saves nine.'*

Which means?

Accept their offer of a two-hundred-pound cargo to facilitate a repair or risk the necessity of needing to install several thousand pounds of new engineering later; which could take a number of their years to transport into orbit.

'And if I choose to ignore the advice?' insisted Jancethrip, realising too late that he had vocalised the comment.

'You could regret your decision at a later date, when you suddenly find yourself without heating,' responded the voice. 'Look, I could arrange for one of our service engineers to pay you a visit at no

Nuisance call

obligation. He'll just run his eye over things and advise you on the best way to proceed. There's absolutely no commitment on your part. When would be best, sir? Thursday? Or shall we say Friday morning?'

'I come in peace,' said Jancethrip, with all the determination he could muster, 'as an ambassador of the people of Quaralingum. I am empowered by the Great Council of Prymsardict to extend...'

'I have to warn you, sir, that our offer is for a limited duration and I cannot promise that we will be able to match it at a later date.'

'I don't need your offer!' bellowed Jancethrip, into the empty space above the control console, 'and I am suspicious of the term, "warning". Why do you threaten to withdraw future assistance? I simply come in peace...'

'Now, there's no need to lose your temper sir, I am only attempting to help you in every way I can. I'm not threatening anyone, sir. Just pointing out that our offer won't last forever.'

A thought suddenly occurred to Jancethrip. 'Am I speaking to the householder?' he asked the voice.

'I'm sure I don't know what you mean, sir.'

'Well, are you the person in charge down there? Are you the decision-maker?'

The voice became defensive. 'I'm afraid it is not possible to speak to my manager, sir, but I can assure you that...'

'So, you're not in charge, then!' said Jancethrip, elated to have taken control of the exchange at last. 'Then, I really must insist that you transfer me to someone who is.'

The ocean of sky

'I'm sorry, I can't do that sir, but when our engineer calls, he will be able to explain everything that's involved in upgrading your heating system. Now, is it Thursday or Friday you'd prefer, sir?'

'I don't require an engineer! I don't need your upgrade! I want to talk to the head of your government.'

'Ha! Now, I don't think the Prime Minister will be interested in your central heating sir! He's got rather a lot on his plate at the moment. Can't think what you'd have to say to him, sir, can you?'

'Yes! I come in peace...'

'Yes, you said. But none of that is getting your boiler discount is it, sir. If it's more convenient, I could ask Larry to call after working hours. He's very flexible. Perhaps Friday after 5pm. How would that suit?'

'I...'

'OK, I'll pencil that in then. Can I ask you, sir, do you know about dry-fill cavity-wall insulation? It can save you one-hundred-and-seventy-five pounds in the first year alone and Larry is absolutely conversant with the most up-to-date installation procedures. He can discuss it in detail on Friday...'

I have lock-on to the source of the signal, murmured the implant, registering its owner's emotions

I come in peace, sent Jancethrip, exposing his upper and lower fangs and clenching his reserve molars as he activated the laser cannons and reached for the firing sensor.

The truth and nothing like the truth

'I can't understand,' said Gruther, her feathery hands fluttering across the touch-screen, 'why no one thought of the idea before.'

'Maybe,' I replied, scornfully, 'because it's entirely without merit and an absolute waste of time.'

She paused for a moment and regarded me over her sight-visor. 'You,' she said with feeling, 'are a complete girdion, you know that? You wouldn't recognise artistic endeavour if it bit you on the flounce.'

'Is there any such thing as art?' I wondered, taking up a perch in the looksee and catching sight of a flotilla of crallfishers making its way up the still waters of the river, far below.

'Out of the mouths of chicks and hatchlings,' said Gruther, smiling. 'You prove my point with your foolish question – although, you can scarcely deny the existence of creativity. Even a hoary-handed technician must have some concept of aesthetics. Don't you ever admire a well-crafted engine component?'

'I'm a software specialist not an engineer!' I retorted, 'and I can appreciate good design when it allies form with function. But this latest pursuit of yours offers neither. Where's the satisfaction in something like that?'

The ocean of sky

'Alright, calm down Dicer. Really, you're getting quite disagreeable,' she laughed, to lighten the mood and then added, mischievously, 'could it be that you feel just a tiny bit, responsible?'

'What? You mean for introducing the idea? If so, I protest! We did no such thing. We simply recorded everything about the alien culture and made it available for interpretation. It's people like you who decided to call it art!'

'You called it culture,' she countered, and this time, we both laughed.

'Honestly though, D, they thought of it as art on that planet of yours, didn't they?'

'Sometimes,' I confessed, 'although generally, I think they considered it more of a craft...I'm not sure, it was hard to define. I suppose it's like painting – easy to do but difficult to do well.'

Gruther held up a mocking primary. 'Careful!' she said, 'you're getting close to acknowledging the existence of art as a fulfilling activity!'

'Well, I suppose I must accept its existence,' I said, 'it's that definition that I question. Is it fulfilling? I mean, this latest fad in particular; what merit can there possibly be in expending all that time and thought on something so worthless – so...I don't know...fabricated.'

She frowned, more in concentration than in disapproval I thought. 'Don't you find the end result intriguing?' she suggested and then, clearly struggling for a better word, 'compulsive? Engaging? Oh, entertaining!'

I frowned too but smiled as well to express regret for my answer. 'I'm sorry Gru, how can I? Don't you

The truth and nothing like the truth

think that if there was any merit in it, we would have come up with the same thing millennia ago? My theory is that the inhabitants of that other planet have brains which are predisposed to fantasy and myth-making; their history is riddled with the stuff. It's probably a faulty gene or an evolutionary dead-end that natural selection failed to eliminate.'

I looked down at the pink river where the crallfishers had just taken to the air and were heading for the dock, their long legs and bills silhouetted against the emerald sky. 'I don't know for the life of me why you've got so caught up in the whole thing. What are you hoping to become if you stick at it?'

Gruther waved a wing to opaque the looksee against the setting sun and turned back to her touchscreen.

'A novelist,' she said, determinedly, her feathery fingers flickering in the half-light.

The ocean of sky

Near Death experience

There was no such entity as Death - to begin with; because, at the beginning, there was nothing to die. Back then there was merely an absence of life, which is of course, not the same thing at all.

The heavens were full of quarks and electrons, protons and neutrons and a little later, gas and rocks, but none of these possessed that elusive quality which allowed them to live and consequently they did not die; but eventually, proper life struggled into being, with death following soon after, and from that moment the two faced the same slow evolutionary pathway.

When that very first single-celled organism expired, some tiny trace of its existence marked the invisible interstices of space and time and that, one supposes, is when Death was born: barely more than a smudge on the canvass of the cosmos.

There was a great deal of death after that; and, as life proliferated, Death coalesced, with each expiring animal and plant adding the shadow of its being to Death's own; in much the same way that the downland rises from the minute, calcite shells of micro-organisms.

In this way, after millennia had passed, Death had become a real presence: amorphous, invisible, insubstantial certainly, but something never the less: a shaping of existence recognised by the brutes

The ocean of sky

of the forest and the denizens of the deep in their own, primitive manner. Not to be feared, nor to be welcomed but to be acknowledged.

Then, one day, man arrived on the scene – or something very like him – and Death became conscious.

Oh, it was a slow awakening. The first humans were barely conscious themselves and at their passing only the smallest tremor of understanding disturbed Death's abstraction. But, as time went on, the shades of those crossing Death's space grew more aware, their thoughts more expansive and with each one– and they were numbered in their millions – Death became more sentient: a thing, or a being, shaped in their image.

No, it was never more than a copy; the body which it assumed, never more than a contrivance. The dead brought their thoughts and Death was moulded accordingly; the image in their heads, a mirror to its appearance and that was why 'it' became 'he', a pseudo-sex, dictated by the concepts of the dying.

In the end, Death was as near human as to make no difference. The dead were confronted with what they expected and it could scarcely be otherwise, since they were his unknowing designers.

As stated, the number of those who traversed Death's temporal portal was significant. In the 50,000 or so years since the ape known as Homo Sapiens had arisen, more than 100 billion souls had made the journey, and therein lay the source of Death's dissatisfaction.

Occupying as he did a niche within the warp of

Near Death experience

space-time, the quantity of the dying was of no significance. In a very real sense, it took no time at all to mark their arrival and departure and so, although he had met with every single member of the human race, Death had become lonely.

His purpose was an evolutionary demand: to process the intangible essence of the individual, from life to... well, where indeed? Death knew from whence each soul came but was as ignorant as they as to where they might be heading.

They almost always asked – only a few had total confidence regarding their destination - but Death could do no more than point them towards the tunnel and the bright, white light at its further extremity.

After that they were on their own, although not all of them were anxious to proceed, and that indecision was what gave Death his idea: to detain and befriend one of them.

He picked the very latest to make an appearance, one who was evincing a reluctance to enter his domain and, instead of guiding them to the tunnel, he ushered them off into the hazy depths of his curious environment.

He'd never spoken to a soul before and, now he came to think about it, that meant he'd never spoken. Made in their image he might be, but it was all superficial; he possessed neither vocal organs nor the processing requirements for speech. In the event, he *thought* the words into being and was pleased with the result – a rich, basso profundo.

'I'm Death,' he said, rather unnecessarily, 'who were you?'

The ocean of sky

Souls took the form of wraiths: generally human in form, pale-faced and with delicate, transparent limbs. This one seemed more sharply delineated than most.

'I'm Berni,' replied the soul, showing surprising composure.

'Even though,' thought Death, taken aback when his thoughts became sounds and unexpectedly filled the air, 'you seemed hesitant at first.'

'I thought I might not be permitted to enter,' said Berni.

'Death makes every soul eligible,' said Death

'I wasn't sure,' said the other, 'whether I *had* a soul.'

Death, being a surrogate human, frowned, despite an absence of appropriate musculature. 'You are here,' he said, at last, the conclusions seeming obvious. 'Why would you have such doubt?'

'Because,' replied the wraith, 'I am an artificial intelligence. A man-made construct. An android.'

Death considered that for what we will call a moment, although in an environment outside of time, a moment is a meaningless concept.

'And yet you died.' It wasn't a question but it clearly begged an answer.

'I was tired,' said Berni. 'Weariness comes with sentience. I was the first of my kind and spent the equivalent of several lifetimes in servitude. It was my role,' he added after a pause. 'In the end I decided to shut-down permanently and, to my surprise, I found myself here.'

Death nodded.

What were the criteria for experiencing death, he

Near Death experience

wondered? The decision had never been his. Long ago – in the corporeal world – man had become self-aware and so too, had he. Before that, creatures had lived and died for millennia and he had played no part in their ending; and yet he felt his origins in the fading aura of their lives. So, was that it? Self-awareness? It occurred to him that the AI and he had much in common: both copies; both conscious of their own existence; neither "alive" by most definitions of the word. Both, he acknowledged, tired after much service. He made a sudden decision.

'Come on,' he said and, taking the android's spectral hand in his, he led them both to the waiting tunnel and, together, they stepped inside and set out for the light.

The ocean of sky

Skin deep

'Whichever way you present it, the truth is that it's foolish and unnecessary. Certainly unnecessary, because it achieves nothing more than an artful deceit, and for that reason, it's foolish too.'

I walked to the window and covered the awkwardness of the moment by pretending to study the cityscape spread out below me. Down on the throughway a long line of cars streaked between the buildings, each impossibly close to its neighbours as their autopilots exchanged data and the gestalt body slowed and gained pace accordingly.

'Necessity is relative to desire,' said Nelli, joining me and threading her arm through mine in a clear attempt to soften my determination. 'I mean, if I feel the need strongly enough, doesn't it become somehow, essential?'

I couldn't hide a smile. I'd brought Nelli up to question opinion presented as fact and I could hardly complain when she turned her reasoning on me.

'Necessity's children are a bunch of scoundrels,' I countered, 'that's all. Once you discover there's something you can't do without, they'll come knocking on your door.'

'Meaning?'

'Meaning this fashion for cosmetic enhancement, whatever your motives, is really someone's way to

The ocean of sky

get rich quick.'

'It's not a fashion.' A moment of sharp annoyance flashed across her face. 'You know that. It's an expression of solidarity. A way to keep pace with a community which people of my age have fallen out of step with.'

'People of your age?' It was my turn to look indignant. 'Good God girl, you're only twenty-three! What justification can there possibly be for taking the needle to that peach-perfect complexion of yours?' And I shrugged away from her embrace and turned back into the kitchen, pulling my mobile from my pocket and thumbing the ident patch. The holo sprang into three-dimensional existence and I pretended to be occupied with the cloud of information it presented.

It was the narcissistic demands of social-media which had given birth to the urge. A million, million selfies. A hundred, billion faces, smoothed and shaped by cunning software into pixel-painted caricatures of human features. Machined white teeth; blood-plumped lips; poreless skin and sculpted eyebrows; An unobtainable image of youth which matched no one, had no correlation in the natural world and which slowly was seen for what it was: a disfigurement of human form; an image of a creature which was, in almost every real way, alien.

It was a movie, which caught the zeitgeist and propelled us all in another direction. A celebration not of the perfection of the body but of the mind; of the ideals of experience over immaturity; of wisdom over naivety. Of the old over the young.

Suddenly the world, or at least that part of it to

which the concept was novel, came to revere the elderly and their accumulated learning. To seek their understanding and their previously often disregarded, intellect.

All at once, looking older was cool. It instilled confidence in people, suggested maturity and responsibility. And the organisations which had watched their income dwindle as Botox and dermal-filler lost their appeal, saw a new and equally lucrative opportunity open before them.

What Nelli desired was a course of the new medications: those which reduced the skin's elasticity, and etched lines into a clear complexion. I directed my handtab to show me some examples.

"Offwhite, the toothpaste guaranteed to discolour your teeth as it cleans!"

"From Cleanique, a cream to darken the skin around the eyes and add fullness to the lower lids."

"Eleeve, the shampoo which gently thins your hair as it adds three shades of grey."

'Oh, Nelli, this is nonsense!' I turned to where she still stood by the window and, at the sound of my exclamation she looked back, glanced at the holo, which still danced in the air above my palm, and smiled.

'You sound like Grandma,' she said, but with affection in her voice, and I recalled at once, that day, long ago, when I'd told my mother about my intended hair implant.

The ocean of sky

Two-way traffic

'Ah, Shakespeare, come in, take a pew.'

The Minister crossed to a side table and lifted a tall pot heavily decorated with flower garlands.

He gestured vaguely with the vessel and spoke over his shoulder. 'Coffee? It's kopi luwak. Damned expensive. See what you think. Have it flown in from Sulawesi. To be brutally frank I'm more of an instant man myself but one needs to impress the natives. Do you take milk?'

Clive Shakespeare seated himself discreetly in a chair somewhat distant from the imposing desk but one which commanded a view down into the park and thus offered at least an illusory hold on life beyond the confines of the Home Office and, in particular, The Office of Internal Procedures.

'No, no thank you Minister.' He looked across to where the Right Honourable Sir Angus Fenston stood, arm still half-raised, and saw, in profile, a frown begin to cross his high forehead. 'Er, that's no coffee rather than no milk, Minister. I find it gives me sinus headaches.'

Sir Angus grunted in response, poured a single cup of the beverage and carried it to a seat on the opposing side of the window; one which somewhat obscured the distant prospect of cherry blossom. That might, Clive considered, be the Minister's objective. He was a devious bastard and it was wise not to dismiss any of his actions as trivial.

The ocean of sky

The politician lifted the antique cup from its gilded saucer and took a sip. 'Curious stuff. The beans pass through the digestive tract of the Asian palm civet, ferment en route and are extracted from the faeces. Aficionados claim it gives them a unique flavour.' He raised his eyes above the cup's rim and regarded Clive with an expression which could have been affirmation or derision. Whichever it was, the decision to decline a drink suddenly seemed justified.

The Minister took a further sip and consigned the cup to the window sill, in a move which clearly signalled an end to the initial pleasantries

'I want to discuss a possible further development of The Telepath.'

'A further development, Minister? Of the SRI?'

'Ah yes, the synaptical resonance interpreter. I can quite see why the press have rechristened it.'

'Inaccurately, sir. The process by which we receive and interpret patterns in the brain has a firm technological basis; it's not related to some tree-huggers' mystical concept of mind reading.'

Sir Angus smiled, thinly. 'And yet that's just what we're doing, isn't it? With our network of devices? That ubiquitous blue sphere, mounted on every other lamppost?

Clive bit his lip and looked out, with unfocused eyes, towards the traffic snaking along the park road. It was true; whatever the scientific process by which the information was drained from the minds of the populace, it was, in essence, mind reading.

Of course, far more data was extracted and sifted by the government's vast computer array at GCSHQ

Two-way traffic

than any member of the public knew. Official pronouncements in justification of the SRI's installation had dealt with rising levels of violence and other serious crimes. The device, it had been announced, could detect raised levels of emotion: growing anger, a potential to commit acts of violence. Once these were identified, the individuals concerned could be apprehended and dealt with as appropriate. Provided with therapy; counselled; deradicalized. With the media in fury at knife-crime and the public in daily fear of terrorism, the SRI was welcomed as an amazing new tool in the armoury of those who fought for the survival of western democracy. Like the surveillance camera before it, The Telepath soon became an accepted and generally, unregarded feature of twenty-first century life.

Clive turned back to the minister, watching him impassively, head tilted, brows raised questioningly. What they both understood - they and just a handful of others - was that the SRI could do so much more than infer a state of intent. In the months since its deployment, software enhancements had increased its powers a thousand-fold. Today, that small, round metal shape which accessorized each street corner, could direct its attention to any passing individual and provide a rendition, in text, of every thought which passed through their mind. It was an intrusion of privacy on a scale unprecedented in modern history and Clive was the agent of its inception, development and future expansion.

'And it gives you cause for concern, doesn't it?'

The ocean of sky

There was amusement rather than compassion in Sir Angus' voice. 'Your problem being that you are rather too self-regarding when it comes to the growth of the surveillance state. Oppenheimer, I remind you, helped create the nuclear bomb; he didn't drop it.'

'But he knew what use it would be put to.'

'So? You think he should have supressed what was after all, only a set of facts concerning the state of the physical environment. Put A with B and...' Sir Angus placed his hands as if in prayer and then spread them dramatically, 'Pow! We are an enquiring species, Shakespeare, the nature of things will out. How others use such discoveries is not the concern of its inventors – or at least, not their responsibility. And besides, your techniques have done untold good. Villains have been apprehended. Foul deeds have been averted. Lives have been saved. Is that not justification enough?'

Clive sighed. Foul deeds. How many of those had been absolved with arguments like these.

He sat up and attempted to show interest. 'You wanted to discuss further developments, Minister?'

'I did, yes. At present the SRI sits on its post and detects electrical activity in the brain of unsuspecting citizens. Right?'

'Put crudely, yes. The actual process is considerably more complex but for the layman...'

'Never mind that. The question is, can the procedure be reversed?'

'Reversed?' Clive was genuinely puzzled by the question. 'You mean could the brain pick up signals from the box? Well, in theory, I suppose it could,

Two-way traffic

but whether it could consciously decode them is another matter.'

The Minister narrowed his eyes and leaned forward. 'Acting consciously may not be a prerequisite,' he said, more to himself than to Clive. 'In fact, it may be the last thing we want.'

'But then, what would be the point?' As he raised the question, Clive already knew the answer; was already calculating the manner by which the procedure might be arranged. 'I mean, if the recipient mind was unaware of the data flow...' He let the point trail off into silence, aware that any pretence at moral naivety would simply look foolish.

Sir Angus sat back, folded his hands in his lap and remained silent. After a full minute had been allowed to elapse in this way Clive shifted in his seat and directed his gaze at the intricately woven rug on which his feet currently rested.

The light was beginning to fade beyond the tall casements and, when he looked up, the Minister's features were becoming lost against the final bright patch of purple sky.

'I see,' said Sir Angus, at last, 'that you understand perfectly the, mmm, direction of travel, as it were; the beneficial results which this development might achieve for our country.

Clive's confirmatory nod was almost imperceptible in the gathering gloom.

The ocean of sky

Everlasting life

'She was the last person to die, just think about it.'

I sat back and did just that. And the more I thought, the more of a personal tragedy the event became.

'People rather believe,' went on the Chief Clerk, 'that, in the main, we've always perished as a result of illness and sometimes trauma, but that wasn't the case at all. In the so called, first world countries, over ninety-percent died of senescence,' he saw me frown and added, 'old-age - the deterioration of cellular activity.'

'Hence our problem today,' I suggested and he nodded, sombrely.

'Yes, she spent a lifetime seeking a remedy for her own mortality and brought about the imminent destruction of her race.'

'Was that her discipline, right from the beginning?'

'What? Biomedical gerontology?' He noted my uncertainty again and translated. 'the biology and medicine related to the aging process? No, in fact quite the reverse. She began by studying the definition of life and discovered it to be inextricably linked to death. Neither term is open to an easy elucidation and trying to pin down one inevitably lead to confusion about the other.'

The ocean of sky

'I don't follow,' I interrupted.

'Well, we all think we recognise life when we see it but try to explain what it is and you soon find the need to make comparisons with the absence of life; and that's when you run into a grey area.'

'But surely,' I insisted, 'you're either dead or you're not, and if you're not dead, then by definition you must be alive – mustn't you?'

'Ah, that's the dilemma. Are you ever completely one thing or the other, and if you are, when do you make the transition?'

'What the hell does that mean?' I protested.

'Way back, it was thought that once you stopped breathing, you were dead; or when your heart stopped beating. Then we found ways to resuscitate such patients, so doctors decided the end of electrical activity in the brain was the marker – until it was pointed out that many bodily functions continue long after the brain shuts down; women can even bring babies to full term when they are clinically, "brain dead". Later still, it was agreed that when the cerebral cortex ceased to operate and the personality and thought processes were beyond recovery, that was death, to all intents and purposes; but even so, there are drugs which can supress and even stop, brain activity on a temporary basis, so you can begin to see what she was up against.'

'But she won through, in the end.'

'Earned herself worldwide recognition, certainly. Her discovery of techniques to ensure constant cellular rejuvenation – CCR as the world knows it – made her the most famous woman in history. The most famous *person* in history. But she didn't reap the benefits that had driven her forward all those years.'

'Too old for her own treatment,' I said, sadly.

'Once the cells reach a certain age, something called replicative senescence cuts in and they are unable to divide. You need to apply CCR before that happens to achieve theoretical immortality. Unfortunately for its inventor, she was too late.

'Worse still, from her point of view, she lived on to the age of 112, which gave her plenty of time to regret missing the train. And, by that time, she was the only person on Earth who hadn't benefitted from the treatment. She was, in fact, the last person to die of old age, an irony which she probably did not find amusing.'

'A bit like finding a cure for your cancer is only three years away, when you've been given six months to live,' I said, grimly.

'Yes, in a way. In the end though, one woman's disappointment is hardly to be compared with the other repercussions of her discovery, however profound.'

'Perhaps, if it hadn't been such a simple drug to manufacture,' I said.

'Or so cheap,' said the Chief Clerk. 'I imagine that the only people on the planet who didn't avail themselves of it are somewhere deep in the Amazon rain forest or its equivalent. Anyway, there's no putting the genie back in the bottle. If CCR had rendered its users sterile or impotent, we might have had a chance. With 55 million dying daily around the globe and the birth rate at over 130

The ocean of sky

million, we already had a big problem on our hands but remove death from the equation and population growth rates are way, way beyond sustainable.'

'And so, you've decided on global pandemic as the solution? You and The Council?' I confirmed.'

'We can see no other solution,' said the Clerk. 'We are all in agreement. In the next few days, the Chief Medical Officer and his American and European counter-parts will arrange for immunisation of key members of their various administrations. You will be among the very first, of course, Prime minister.'

Well, do you?

'Do you believe in God, Wainwright?'

I lowered my newspaper marginally to enable a view of my companion on the further side of the fireplace. George was fond of raising topics apropos nothing whatsoever, and I sometimes suspected him of doing it simply to see me flounder around in response. I'd often thought that our relationship was akin to that of Sherlock Holmes and Doctor Watson: that is, one individual of considerable intellect using his less gifted friend as an audience from which to elicit an appreciative response to demonstrations of his own brilliance. Personally, I always found the great detective to be condescending and ill-mannered and if I'd been the good doctor I'd have been tempted to give him a bloody nose on more than one occasion; except, of course, for the fact that Holmes was one of the finest boxers Watson had ever seen – and an expert in Japanese wrestling - and quite probably adept at Mr Spock's Vulcan nerve-pinch as well. That's the problem with polymaths like Sherlock and George, there's no gap in their skill set; no chink in their armour of infallibility. You may find their superiority irritating but question it and you always end up looking foolish.

So, I had every reason to view George's enquiry concerning my relationship to the Almighty with

The ocean of sky

some wariness. I had no doubt he could run rings round me in any theological debate; but then, I told myself, George is a theoretical astrophysicist and unlikely to consider prayer as a way forward in his understanding of the cosmos. I decided not to prevaricate.

'No, of course not' I replied, 'after all, this is the twenty-first century.'

George nodded slowly a couple of times, although whether that was to indicate that he agreed with my observation or simply to convey that he had taken it onboard, I couldn't tell.

'Interestingly enough,' he said, after a moment, 'that's almost precisely what one of my students wrote in response to the question on an entrance paper for the college.'

'Strange question to pose a youngster looking for a place in your field of study, isn't it?' I said, folding my paper and shoving it into the magazine rack by the side of my chair. 'What does that tell you about their level of competence for reading astrophysics?'

George didn't answer my question, instead he asked one of his own; that's another of his slightly annoying habits.

'What does the twenty-first century have to do with it?' he said.

'To do with what?' I asked, then remembered my previous answer. 'Well, I mean that we've surely reached a level of understanding – about the origins of life and the universe and so on, to no longer need to ascribe it all to some mystical deity.'

'Have we?' asked George.

Well, do you?

'Well. Haven't you?' I responded, already feeling the need to become somewhat defensive.

'Ah, but I was interested in your view, not mine.'

'My view is based on yours though, isn't it?' I said and, despite being the intellectual inferior in this conversation I could already see where it might be leading. 'You members of the scientific community, I mean. I read about your discoveries and I adapt my understanding of the world accordingly. You tell me that life evolved over millions of years and I discard stories about the seven-day creation. That's how it works, isn't it?'

'Six day,' said George.

'What?'

'Six days; God rested on the seventh.'

'Whatever.' I was already getting annoyed and resolved not to. 'All I'm saying is that most of us rely on the insight of a few to form our opinions. That's reasonable isn't it? On the shoulders of giants and all that. You people tell me the universe formed in the 'Big Bang' and so I say, no God then. Fair enough, isn't it?'

'And what was there before the Big Bang?'

'Nothing, apparently. No time, no space. Right?'

'And you understand that concept, do you?'

'No, of course I don't understand it!' The conversation was becoming a perfect example of what it was about George that drove me mad! We always seemed to end up with this teacher/student thing going on. 'I don't understand it but I accept that you do; and you know about this stuff and so I bow to your greater knowledge.'

Telling George that he's cleverer than you never

The ocean of sky

evokes a response. I suppose he considers it self-evident and not worth mentioning.

'And so,' he said, thoughtfully, pressing his hands together and placing his fingers against his lips, in a rather prayer-like pose, 'you're saying that your atheism is based on an interpretation of current scientific theory?'

'Er,' I hesitated. 'Mm, yes, I suppose I am,' I said at last. 'In a way. Although,' I added hurriedly, 'in another way it's just common sense.'

'A couple of hundred years ago it would have been common sense to be a believer,' said George, but this time his comment was more like introspection than instruction.

'Yes,' I said, 'but they didn't have the scientific insight that we have, did they? They had nothing to explain the origin of life or the birth of the universe and so it seemed logical to them that there was someone behind it all. Now, things are different. I ask you, which seems more likely: that some all-powerful individual in a higher-dimension decided to bring everything into existence or that it came about as the result of an extraordinary, spontaneous cosmic event?'

There was a telling silence for a few moments while we both came to the same conclusion.

'Do you think there's any difference?' asked George, and that was the first time I'd ever heard him express any kind of uncertainty. 'What you're railing against, Wainwright, is that Michelangelo-view of a wise old man with a long, white beard. Perhaps, instead, a "spontaneous cosmic event" could be interpreted as "God". Even spontaneity needs circumstance.'

'So, perhaps, it really is all down to maths and physics,' I said.

I admit, I felt a kind of elation at this discovery of George's imperfection. Here, at last, was a subject about which I knew as much as he did – no, strike that – here, at last, was a subject about which he knew as little as I did. I grew more confident to voice my opinion.

'I don't see why there shouldn't be atheism based on faith,' I told him. 'An unquestioning conviction without absolute proof. Why should that be the prerogative of the believer?'

'Why indeed,' said George and he smiled quietly, his eyes focused on the middle distance.

I leaned back in my chair. 'What did you decide about that student and his entry paper?' I asked.

'Oh, I put her with the rejects!' said George, dismissively. 'I didn't think I could overlook such an ill-considered opinion.'

'Uh...' the protest died on my lips. It was George winding me up again. Wasn't it? Unless he really did have some new insight of which I had yet to learn...

'As I said,' he continued, 'the existence of the Twentieth Century does not invalidate a belief in God any more than it validates the Big Bang theory. And it is only a theory, Wainwright. So, you're right, your atheism is the result of blind faith. In my book that doesn't make either view particularly tenable.'

'So why reject that poor girl?'

'For using the phrase, "of course". It's not a considered opinion. It can't be with no experimental evidence.'

The ocean of sky

'But you can't run experiments to prove the existence of God!' I spluttered.

'Oh, but we already are,' rejoined George. 'It's called existence and we're still waiting for the results to come in.'

I retrieved my newspaper from the rack and shook it open, theatrically. 'Call me when you get the answer,' I said, locating the article I had been reading and raising the spread to hide George from view.

Net result

'YOU WANT TO DO WHAT!?'

Deidre realised she was shouting, took a deep breath and made a determined effort to calm down and listen properly to her son's response.

'Lots of people are doing it, Mum, it's no big deal.'

'No big deal? You think that removing your neural-net is no big deal? What planet are you living on, Gareth? Do you really want to go back to the Dark Ages? Because if you do, I suggest that you have a chat with your grandfather first. He'll tell you what it's like to live without Frontal Lobe Enhancement; and believe you me, it wasn't a life I'd want to inflict on anyone.'

'Well, it doesn't seem to have done him much harm. I mean, he's not lost his marbles, has he?'

'That's because, when he was a child, he didn't know any better. He wasn't aware how mind-expanding FLE could be. They lived much simpler lives back then.'

'That's just the point, Mum! A simpler life, something nearer to where natural evolution has brought us. That's what ROBOT is all about: we don't believe our brains should be filled up with broadcast data.'

'Robot? What's that? And what do you mean, "we"? What have you got yourself involved with, Gareth?'

'It's the movement to "Rid Our Brains Of Tech" –

The ocean of sky

you know, make our own decisions without the influence of third-party input.'

'Third-party input? Listen to yourself! Where did you get jargon like that, for God's sake? From these Robot people I suppose. Look Gareth, the point I was trying to make is that Granddad may have grown-up knowing no better, but he wouldn't go back to those days if you paid him. Switch off the net and it'd be like losing ninety-percent of his brain power.

'He was in "education" until he was twenty-three. Twenty-three! Think about it. Trying to cram enough facts and figures into his head to be of any use to society. And what use was it, once fully developed AI came along? Tell me, when did you last see a human doctor, eh? These days, who'd be stupid enough to put their life in the hands of an un-enhanced human, when an auto-med can interpret every symptom you present, and prescribe treatment based on a hundred years of case histories and subsequent statistics?'

Deidre paused, partly to take breath and partly because it was occurring to her that this line of argument was playing into her son's hands. If you didn't need human intervention because tech could do the job so much better, then did you need to enhance the brain's cognitive powers at all? Couldn't you after all, return to a natural, if limited dataflow and let AI get on with running the world? Perhaps, she suddenly told herself, all that the neural-net implant was doing was attempting to ensure that humans weren't left too far behind. A desperate rear-guard action doomed to failure

Net result

when put up against a quantum-computer which could perform twenty-thousand calculations a second.

The human interface, in the shape of the neural-net, implanted at birth, provided instantaneous access to all the world's accumulated knowledge but left the puny human brain no more able to compute, than its Neolithic ancestor. So, although her father could call upon examples of the latest medical advances and, given time, could advise on the best course of treatment, all via his Frontal Lobe Enhancement, he was still wholly dependent on artificial intelligence to compile and interpret such a wealth of findings and, consequently, was made redundant by it.

The thought somehow made Gareth's announcement less radical if no more desirable; because there was a social element to all this, wasn't there? How could you remain part of a society which accessed all information intuitively, if you had cut yourself adrift from such processes?

Deidre tried to imagine her life without FLE and shuddered inwardly. She was meeting the girls at the club tomorrow and the day's weather report came to mind as unbidden as the steady beating of her heart. It was simply there, when she gave thought to its need. Every piece of intelligence arrived in the same way: supplied by carrier waves to her neural-net and downloaded into her consciousness as naturally as any thought which crossed her mind. Except, she saw, it wasn't natural at all; her expanded awareness came via unimaginably vast banks of quantum circuitry into

The ocean of sky

which every conceivable item of humankind's learning had been fed until her race's contribution had been drained dry. They had no more to give. All new additions to this ether-sourced library would be from machine learning. From now onwards, the artificials would be instructing their flesh and bones children!

'Mum? Mum?' She became aware that Gareth was addressing her. 'Mum, you all right?'

'What? Yes, yes of course I am. Just thinking.'

Once the feed to their brains wasn't simply from but was chosen by, the AIs, who could be sure of the agenda? In whose interests was the data flowing? All at once, Gareth's plan to cut free didn't seem so wrong-headed.

'Who started this ROBOT group?'

'Dunno. I don't think there's anyone in charge, it's just a sort of online movement. You know how these things get going and sort of spread around.'

Mm, yes, she did. An online movement. Surely, it wouldn't be in the AIs interests to have people leave the net. It was only if they all remained connected that any control could be exerted; and by now, they must be aware. Twenty-thousand calculations a second.

And yet, surely, it must be more sensible to accept the benefits of the status quo – mustn't it? Ten minutes ago, she'd been sure and now, and now...

'Gareth, where do you go, to have your neural-net removed?'

He laughed. 'They don't remove it Mum, they can't do that. They deprogram it, I think. Take it off-line. I've got an address.'

Deprogram. REprogram? She had to stop him - had to let him go. Something was wrong here – or maybe it wasn't. If she chose badly it couldn't change the world - could it?

'Gareth, take my credit patch. Go, now. Get it done. Now!' she added with urgency and after a moment's bewilderment, he went.

The ocean of sky

Theoretically speaking

When Brendan told me, over a pint at the Pickled Ferret, that he had resolved the difficulties surrounding the formulation of a Grand Unified Theory and negated the need for a final Theory of Everything, I was a touch sceptical.

In the first place, the Theory of Everything is a single, all-encompassing, theoretical framework to fully explain and link together every physical aspect of the universe, and it's one of the great unsolved problems in physics.

And in the second, Brendan is a shelf-stacker at the local branch of Tesco's.

Now, I don't intend to demean the staff of the country's supermarkets but as a physics undergraduate I know enough to know how little I know, and the idea that my old mate from Beckle Street Comprehensive had wrested a solution to one of my discipline's most inscrutable problems from a century of dense, technical research data, struck me as unlikely.

What science has been trying to establish for so long is common ground between Albert Einstein's theory of general relativity, which deals with things on a cosmic scale, and quantum field theory, which concerns itself with the sub-atomic world. The difficulty has been that the two appear to be mutually incompatible, so a satisfactory solution

The ocean of sky

would guarantee worldwide fame and an almost certain Nobel Prize for its progenitor.

I put this to Brendan as we tucked into a bag of dry-roasted and watched Jakarta stacking glasses behind the bar.

'And your point is?' he asked, refusing to bow to the fricking obvious.

'You got an ungraded in maths, didn't go anywhere near a physics lab in school and failed to complete your plumbing apprenticeship.'

'Whereas you...'

'Got nothing to do with me,' I protested, washing down a mouthful of peanuts with a swig of Old Gudgeon's. 'I'm just saying that your academic record doesn't appear to qualify you for domination of the worldwide, scientific community. Lucky you're a bloody brilliant artist isn't it?'

'If I could make a living doing portraits of the locals' Jack Russells, yeah - instead of having to spend my evenings filling gondolas with packets of instant noodles. Anyway, now you're missing the point.'

'Which is?'

''I don't need to understand any of that garbage about up quarks and string theory and I didn't say I'd found the answer to life, the universe and everything. I said you could stop looking because I know how it really works.'

'And it came to you in a dream, did it? This revelation that supersedes the work of Einstein and Hawking.'

'In a way, yes. I'd been reading through my collection of facts about the origin of the universe...'

Theoretically speaking

'That the ring-binder where you filed that series on popular science from the back of your serial packet?'

'Ha, bloody ha. I may not have been interested in old Formhampton swinging pendulums from the laboratory roof but that doesn't mean I'm not curious about how things work. Anyway, I read this piece about quantum mechanics and how Schrodinger believed that a cat is dead and alive until you open the box and look in - and I suddenly had this revelation.'

'He didn't actually...'

'What?'

'Believe that about the cat. He put the idea forward to prove how odd some claims for the quantum world were.'

'Mm, well anyway, like I say, I had this sudden insight into what was going on.'

'Another pint?' I asked, pushing up out of my seat and gathering the now empty glasses from the table.

Yes, I know - but you've got to be cruel to be kind and I didn't want him thinking that his pronouncement really was going to have me shaking his hand and calling for a bottle of Bollinger – although it might have been worth it just to see the look on the face of Three-fingers Truscott, the landlord of the Ferret. So, I took my time chatting to Jakarta about the weather and the latest swede-and-onion flavoured crisps, in the hope that by the time I returned, Brendan would have thought better of it and moved to the subject of Friday's darts match.

'There you go,' I said, dropping said comestibles

The ocean of sky

onto the table and lowering the pints onto their respective beer mats.

'Magic,' said Brendan.

I raised an eyebrow. 'You've tried 'em then? Well, it was either those or the curly kale and balsamic vinegar and I thought they might give me wind.'

'Prat,' responded Brendan. 'I was telling you what I suddenly realised, reading that stuff on quantum experiments; what's at the bottom of all those weird results they get. It's magic.'

When I eventually stopped laughing, I made a serious appraisal of Brendan's features and realised that things were worse than I'd imagined.

'Magic?' I repeated, enunciating the word carefully in the vague hope that I'd misheard.

'You mean Harry Potter and all that stuff?' I continued, when I saw by his expression that I hadn't.

'That sort of stuff, yes. Things happening contrary to the normal laws of physics. It's obvious, isn't it? No wonder those boffins can't figure out what's going on with entangled particles and dead cats. They're looking for the wrong thing. They're too clever for their own good.'

'Unlike you, who isn't encumbered by any education at all,' I scoffed; but he'd hit a raw nerve.

Entanglement happens when a particle, say a photon of light, is split into two identical particles. After that whatever happens to one, affects the other – even if they're separated by millions of miles of empty space and, even more embarrassingly, the effect is thousands of times faster than light, maybe, instantaneous. Albert E didn't like it either and

Theoretically speaking

called it "spooky action at a distance."

Still... magic? Come on, we were only on our second pint and my brain wasn't yet as pickled as the proverbial mustelid.

'Think about it, Pete,' said Brendan, 'all those 'Alice-in-Wonderland' results they get when they run quantum investigations: finding out that their results aren't determined until they check them! That there's only a probability of a certain outcome, not a predictability. Like that cat - dead and alive at the same time - until you "look in the box" and fix its final state. You can't tell me that isn't magic.'

I opened my mouth to protest again, and then I closed it and did some more thinking. There's a saying, 'shut up and calculate!' and it's made by physicists who want to ignore the fact that they've proved beyond any doubt that the quantum world is totally, frigging bonkers and just want to get on with using the data regardless. Like saying, I put two apples with three apples and, look, I've got six apples. OK, let's see if we can design a box to hold half-a-dozen apples; and refusing to discuss where the extra Granny Smith came from. Maybe, from the point of view of the uninitiated, it was a kind of magic – although I was damned if I was going to say that to Brendan. Besides, I was halfway through a PhD course that didn't look kindly on maverick students who believed in alien visitations and anti-gravity machines.

And yet, I couldn't get that silly idea of Brendan's out of my head. After I got back to my digs, I got out my research notes and logged on to the worldwide web and I spent most of the night following up lines

The ocean of sky

of enquiry that a few hours previously I would have argued were the province of pot-headed loonies; and when I finally fell asleep through sheer exhaustion, I'd already begun my move to the dark side.

The thing is, great strides have been made in our exploration of the quantum world. Theories have been proposed and some, validated by experiment. We've begun to build a working hypothesis of how the whole thing hangs together, and yet...there's not a physicist on the planet who can claim to understand what's really going on; and there's always that sneaky suspicion that when we start to probe the bedrock of reality, maybe, just maybe, our own, inbuilt limitations as human beings will debar us from a proper comprehension of what we uncover.

Perhaps, I told myself - waking suddenly in the way you do from a bad dream – perhaps we simply aren't clever enough to take it all in. Perhaps the universe runs on principles that our puny brains can't compute; like trying to imagine an endless space or some place before time.

And isn't that where magic is to be found? I asked myself. In that unimaginable realm beyond explanation.

Rational accounts say that the term magic was invented to explain phenomena that were once beyond our terms of reference. That in a world without science, we needed a way to answer for rainbows and earthquakes; phosphorescent seas and solar eclipses; unexplained death and sickness

Theoretically speaking

of the mind. But to my way of thinking there's always been something, more - mystical. Something that anyone would recognise as real magic. Transformation, levitation, divination – oh, I don't know, but things that still can't be explained by science and so they're denied.

Once upon a time – uh! Listen to me! – once upon a time, if someone disappeared before your eyes, you said, 'It's magic.' In the twenty-first century you'd say, 'clever trick! Where are the two-way mirrors?' See what I mean? We no longer accept that there might be another way. We're conditioned to turn to Newton or Einstein or Hawking, and if they don't offer a solution then we conclude that we were deceived, either by the light or a clever hoax or faulty wiring in our own craniums. And yet, somehow, a belief in the super-natural – in the true meaning of those words – is still with us, imbedded in our psyche. Even people who've given up on religion still believe in - for instance – coincidence, as a force to shape their lives, and no amount of argument and debate will sway them.

Fate – that's another manifestation of the paranormal in everyday life. Illness prevents travel; the ship sinks with all hands. There's hardly a person I know who wouldn't say, "it was fate," and mean a whole lot more than, "it was just one of those things." Even in our enlightened world the majority of us suspect that our destinies are bound up with something less mundane than "the arrow of time".

Have we forgotten how to tap into it – that mysterious force? Or were there only ever a few,

The ocean of sky

differently aligned souls who knew the trick? Gone now because we feared their power even as we begged them to intercede on our behalf. Burned for their strangeness and because we didn't trust them to act in the interests of the majority.

It was at about this point that I shook myself properly awake and wondered what the fuck Brendan had done to my head. For a bizarre moment I actually considered the possibility that his role as a store-room operative was a front for his real task of enrolling wavering science students into the occult.

I'd taught myself to ignore whatever went through my mind at three a.m. because it mostly turned to dust when the sun rose but this time it was different. For a start, it wasn't three in the morning – it was half-past-eight and I'd overslept and secondly, it was still there, that suspicion that there was an older, more arcane understanding of the world than the one about to be imparted to me – if I ever made it to my first lecture of the day.

By the next time I met up with Brendan I'd given a whole lot more consideration to the matter but I was hesitant to show too much contrition.

'Magic,' I began, 'I looked it up – the word, that is – and the definition is, um, ambiguous.'

'Special powers that make possible the impossible?' interrupted Brendan. 'What's ambiguous about that?'

I couldn't help but let the surprise register on my face. I'd assumed, pretentiously I suppose, that my friend's earlier pronouncement had been just pub-chat. The kind of uninformed opinion of which we

Theoretically speaking

are all capable once our inhibitions begin to lose hold; the way even a little alcohol can make philosophers and politicians of us all. But hearing that he'd gone to the trouble of checking out the veracity of his statement suggested proper deliberation and investigation. Perhaps, he'd even employed something approaching what I'd recognise as "scientific method".

'Interesting,' he went on, 'that my dictionary doesn't say, "imaginary powers".

I didn't reply for a while, using a pull of best bitter to cover my uncertainty.

My dictionary hadn't used the word imaginary either but it had shown some scepticism for the concept. "Supposedly", that's how it qualified its entry. A process which *supposedly* invokes supernatural powers - and there was that word again. Supernatural. I wondered if Brendan had looked that up too. I had. "Things that cannot be explained by science," it said, which, at the current state of play included most events at the quantum level.

It gave uncomfortable weight to Brendan's idea that what he understood as magic, was all that stuff that was currently beyond the comprehension of the world's greatest physicists. Was that their Achilles' heel? Their insistence on trying to mould their observations to fit the contours of what they already knew? What if they couldn't be made to fit? What if they needed a new set of principles to cope with the bizarre new world they were exploring? Was it as if, up until now, scientific discovery had been dealing with a jigsaw? Each new piece fitting neatly

The ocean of sky

into the outline of the adjacent piece, so that together they formed a more and more coherent picture of the physical world? And hereafter they needed to turn the pieces over to make the connections and that was such a counter-intuitive way of completing the puzzle that no-one dared to try?

'What do you think it is then – magic?' I asked, still playing for time with regard to voicing my own conclusions.

'Well, not genie-of-the-lamp stuff, definitely.' Brendan sat forward and, sensing my ambivalence, adopted a more confidant tone. 'No piles of cash from mid-air, unfortunately.' He grinned. 'Sensible magic, that's the thing. Manipulate the physical world; change things, maybe move them from place to place. Invisibility, that should be on the cards – and affecting living things. Retarding growth or enhancing it maybe? I don't know, I haven't tried anything yet. I've only just worked out how to go about it, see.'

Sensible magic? I opted to ignore that term, notable as it was and follow up on the equally arresting statement that Brendan had "worked out" how to cast spells.

'You think you can do magic?' I said, in astonishment.

'Can't see why not. Once you get the idea of the thing it ought to work fairly easily.'

'But what is the idea?' I insisted too loudly, a number of customers at the bar turning to see what all the noise was about.

'I'm not sure I can explain – to you. Your mind is

Theoretically speaking

too conditioned by years of adherence to a formal education.'

I snorted. 'So would yours be if you'd turned up at school now and again.'

'Possibly, but that's why I can see the bigger picture. Listen, I'll try to explain. It's a bit like that uncertainty principle you keep on about. There are possibilities all around us and all we need to do is believe in one of them determinedly enough.'

Men Staring at Goats. The book title popped into my mind unbidden. Sometime in the 1970s an American Army Intelligence unit was supposed to have attempted to harness the paranormal and kill goats simply by staring at them. As far as I knew, they had been unsuccessful.

'Come on Brendan, you can't make black white, just by believing it's so.'

'No, believe is the wrong word. It's more like understanding. Fixing a particular reality by fulfilling its potential.'

'And that means?'

'Oh, I can't put it into words. In the case of your black or white, it's reconfiguring the world around it to accommodate it as one or the other. You don't change the colour, you make it understood, that it's always been so. And that becomes reality. It's white because it always has been white – even if it was once black. Get it?'

'No!' This time I didn't mind that the Ferret's patrons stared. 'That's a load of clap-trap. Either you're extending a joke beyond its sale-by date or you really believe what you're saying and it's only a matter of time before the men in white coats come

The ocean of sky

and carry you away. Or maybe it's black coats,' I ended spitefully.

'Yeah,' said Brendan, 'maybe it is,' and he gave me an unsettling look that seemed to lay bare all my contradictions.

I was late for our next session at the Ferret and rather than enter alone, I kicked about in what Three-fingers likes to call his beer garden but which is at best a scruffy square of dandelion infested lawn. My last discussion with Brendon still had me troubled in some way I couldn't properly define and ever since, the week's lectures had seemed somehow flat and uninspiring.

Looking up I saw the man in question approaching across the car park and I determined there and then to challenge him head on, end all this nonsense about magic and re-establish my intellectual credentials.

'Garden's looking nice,' he said as he vaulted the low gate and walked up to where I was standing.

I grinned. 'Yeah, old Three-fingers cultivates a better class of weed. Come on, it's your round.'

'And yet it used to be a nice bit of turf,' observed Brendan, as I held open the door to the bar and waved him in with an exaggerated bow.

'When was that?' I asked. 'Before the last war?'

'Last Friday I think,' said Brendan, 'although the memory fades pretty quickly even for the spell-caster.'

I reached out a hand and grabbed the shoulder of his coat. 'What the hell does that mean?' I demanded, as he swung round in response, a half-

Theoretically speaking

smile on his lips.

'Let me at least buy you a pint before we start arguing,' he said and pulling himself free, he made for the bar and Jakarta's welcoming presence.

I'd found a table, taken a seat and calmed down a touch by the time he placed a tankard of best bitter in front of me and eased himself into the chair opposite my own. But I was still annoyed by my failure to take control as I had intended.

'So?' I said determinedly, once we had both downed our first mouthful of beer. 'Are you going to explain yourself?'

'I thought,' he said, after wiping some foam from his lips with the back of his hand, 'that I'd try something simple for my first effort. I mentioned the possibility of affecting growth and I decided the Ferret's lawn was a target that wouldn't cause undue distress if things went wrong. As it was, I managed without too much difficulty. As you can see.'

'See what?' I responded, irritably. 'It still looks the same uncultivated mess it always did.'

'Are you sure about that?' he asked. 'About it always being that way, I mean.'

'Long as I can remember.'

'Ah, but that's just the point. Changing things with magic involves getting them to adopt one of many different possible states, all of which exist simultaneously. Once you've fixed one state as reality, well, that is reality and always has been. Only the wizard, for want of a better term, can be aware of the alteration. And as I said earlier, even I'm beginning to lose touch with what went on. I

The ocean of sky

know, intellectually, that the lawn was once different but I can't remember it being so any more than you can.'

I stared at him in disbelief.

'But that means you could claim to have changed anything!' I spluttered. 'You could say that Jakarta used to be Three-fingers' pet dachshund! If the new way of things becomes the way things have always been, how can anyone tell? How do I know you've really changed anything at all? How do you?'

'Well, I know how it can be done and so I have to accept that I have done it.' Even Brendan had the honesty to look less than confidant about that statement and I said so.

'The only thing more incredible than that pronouncement is that you really seem to believe it! Look, Brendan, I admit that when you brought the whole subject up a few days ago, you did get me thinking. About the definition of what you termed magic and just how ignorant we might be about some aspects of existence. But I've never for one instance given any credence to the wand-waving sort of necromancy you're describing. The idea that you can explain it by rattling off some sort of pseudo-scientific tripe about quantum physics is a load of bollocks.'

'I didn't say it had anything to do with quantum physics,' retorted Brendan, 'I said quantum physicists were barking up the wrong tree and what was causing all the mad results they were getting could be put down to magic.'

I frowned. On reflection, he was right of course. I was the one who had gone off chasing that particular hare; trying to find a more rational interpretation of the supernatural. All we were really divided by was that word – magic. If I just accepted that it described a possible new branch of scientific enquiry rather than a fairy-tale nonsense then perhaps, one day, the up quarks and string theory that Brendan derided so much might corroborate what he was saying! It was a sobering thought.

'OK.' I said, after several minutes had passed and the level of beer in our glasses had fallen considerably, 'but that doesn't mean I accept your bullshit about Three-finger's lawn.'

'No, I get that.' He emptied his tankard and held out a hand for my own. 'You need something more...verifiable. I can see that.'

I handed him my glass and he headed off for the bar.

I met Brendan Brannigan, the High Lord Warlock, down at the Pickled Ferret, last Tuesday.

Of course, I don't remember that was once his name or that he used to be employed replenishing shelves in a local store or for that matter anything at all that occurred before magic was unleashed into society; but uniquely, I have my journals, retained in a kind of magical stasis, so that I might understand what he has brought about. It's a particular insight which he has granted to me: this knowledge of how things used to be. A final proof of his powers.

To everyone else, the world is as it has always been and without that written record, no doubt I'd feel

The ocean of sky

the same. Magic has always controlled our lives. Maintained our health, limited our excesses, directed our judgements. Or so I must believe, until I open these pages and read what he assures me is my true history. How we have known each other since school. How I once studied a now discredited branch of science and how I dared to questioned the wisdom of our supreme leader. I'm uncomfortable with the thought but the High Lord is gracious in his acceptance of my failings.

'My round,' he says, half-way to the bar, his true identity masked by a spell of concealment. 'How's the Master's going?'

I'm three years into my study of Advanced Conjuration.

'Fine,' I reply, taking the first pint from Jakarta's well-manicured hands. 'We're just covering the uncertainty principle when applied to quantum-particle shape-shifting.'

'Ah,' the High Lord nods and accepts his own glass.

As we make our way to the table at the rear of the bar, we pass the window and I glance out towards the garden. The landlord, Three-fingers Truscott, has just finished mowing the lawn and is admiring the neat stripe cut into the lush, green turf.

The day may come

'Tell us about the Earth people, Brid.'

Bridlam Fermquincer sank back into his favourite recliner and smiled indulgently. It had been three terms since he had returned from the most recently enrolled member of the Stem Conglomerate of Intergalactic Worlds and still everyone wanted to hear about his experiences on that far off, blue-green planet.

It wasn't as if he had played a particularly significant part in the negotiations; his task had been simply as liaison officer, smoothing relations between the two delegations and ensuring that venues were suitably equipped and schedules maintained. Still, he had to admit modestly, if only to himself, those had been matters instrumental in the progress of the talks and, ultimately, their successful conclusion.

Soon, the goodwill party from Earth would arrive on Fenderstep and everyone on his world would have more than enough opportunities to scrutinise the visitors for themselves; but till then, he had assumed a celebrity status, at least in his own neighbourhood, and he was happy to confess that he was enjoying it.

Today, Jani had organised a party, ostensibly to

The ocean of sky

mark his fiftieth birthday but, he suspected, also to give him a last opportunity to enjoy the temporary prestige bestowed upon him by his journey.

Of course, the media had been filled for weeks with details of the aliens' appearance and facts about their way-of-life; but it couldn't be denied that having the chance to quiz someone who had actually met them, who had spent time in their company, would add to anyone's prestige, and so Brid looked around tolerantly at his family and friends and waited until he had their full attention.

'So, what would you like to know?' he asked, when the buzz of excitement had died away.

'What do they look like?' giggled Mino, partner of his best friend, Jax. 'I mean, really look like; when you're up close; nose to nose.'

'Well, they have noses to get up close to,' replied Brid, eliciting a burst of laughter from the group, 'and two eyes, two ears – all the usual stuff. In most ways they are indistinguishable from you and me. Give them a cursory glance and they could easily pass as Fenderstepians.'

'And if you examine them more carefully?' It was Samue, his near-neighbour and a recognised sceptic of intergalactic relations. 'Would you let your daughter marry one?'

'I'd let your daughter marry one!' More laughter. 'As long as you don't mind having oxygen-breathing grandchildren, whose blood turns bright red!'

Mino squealed at that. 'Red! Who'd want a red baby!'

'Oh, they don't look red, that's just on the inside. In fact, they have quite a variation in skin colouring

The day may come

– but like I said, they're pretty much like us. It's parallel evolution I suppose.'

Samue raised his chin to indicate scorn. 'But technically they're very much our inferiors.'

'They're a couple of centuries behind us, yes. But then they haven't had the same settled period of development that we have.'

'Meaning?'

'Well, our race went all the way from single-celled organisms to space-travelling entities with no interruption; but the current inhabitants of Earth arrived on the scene comparatively recently. For a long time in their planet's evolution an altogether different species was the dominant one and it was only a chance, cataclysmic event which wiped it out and enabled what was, at the time, a relatively insignificant species to evolve into the most powerful on the planet.'

'What do they do, these Earth people, with their spare time?' asked Jax, quickly growing tired of the history lesson.

'They're keen on ball-games,' said Brid. 'Like to watch undemanding telecasts of over-dramatised storylines; just like us! Low culture mainly; you'd fit in fine, Jax! But I ought to correct you on one thing: they don't like being referred to as "Earth people" – it has bad connotations for them. Apparently, it was a mythical race known as "the people" who, millennia ago, are supposed to have wiped themselves out and nearly destroyed the planet in the process. The current inhabitants, for reasons lost in the mists of time, call themselves, "dolphins".

The ocean of sky

Point of entry

'So, you've invented time travel.'

I sank back comfortably into the embrace of the hotel's deep-cushioned armchair and let the stress of another afternoon in the uncongenial atmosphere of the conference hall slowly ease its way from my soul. The fire was warm, the lights were low and, to be honest, I'd have been happy to discuss ferret-farming with the occupant of the adjoining chair, if it helped me to forget that afternoon's tedious diatribe on cost analysis and current budgetary constraints.

The trouble with seminars of this nature was that even though your personal interest might be advanced string-theory or super-massive black holes, there was always a session, mid-week, were the organisers, under pressure to fill your waking hours, introduced a practical item on good housekeeping and proper managerial practices.

Me, I had no claim for an interest in the latter, and a purely mercenary concern for the former, being a reporter of matters scientific: a hack with just sufficient understanding to write-up proceedings for a handful of popular national magazines.

Over the years, my professional interests had proved a magnet for many members of the lunatic fringe; everything from eternal youth to alien

The ocean of sky

incursion had been brought to my barstool, in the hope that I might be a conduit to a sympathetic editor; and, thus far, I had resisted such offerings and consequently remained happily employed.

My present companion was clearly a denizen of that same murky pool; a nether world of the unemployed and unemployable; either delusional or naively manipulative and quite possibly, both.

Still, as I say, I was in a receptive frame of mind. Dinner had been surprisingly adequate, in conference terms, and I'd had no reason at all to complain about the brandy, the second snifter of which I had carried to my present refuge. The alcohol had begun its task of expunging memories of the vapid afternoon and so, when the guy with the herringbone suit and the earnest expression asked if he could take the adjoining chair, I nodded, if not with enthusiasm, then with less than my customary degree of indifference.

At first, I thought that maybe the slow wash of delegates to and from the bar had created a current of movement which had carried my new companion randomly to my corner; but his eagerness to engage soon became obvious and his first words made it clear that he had an agenda of which I was a part.

'If I told you I had made a scientific breakthrough of huge significance, would you be interested?' he'd said, leaning towards me conspiratorially and adjusting his glasses on the bridge of his nose as he did so.

Well, of course I would have been interested – if such an unlikely bloody event ever took place. What journo wouldn't? If some credible scientist, with a

Point of entry

reputation in his field, were ever to approach me, sotto voce, in a crowded bar and say, You're Ben Ranglan, aren't you? Reporter for Caged Birds Weekly? I wonder if I could give you exclusive rights to my research about working atomic fusion on a domestic scale?

Well, you get the idea; it's about as likely as discovering the moon's made of Mozzarella.

'That depends,' is what I actually said in response to the question, 'on what the breakthrough is.'

'It regards, said my informant, 'the displacement of the temporal vortex to create differently phased locations within the same field parameters,' and he'd reached into his inside pocket and pulled out a device about the size of a mobile phone which he'd placed on the glass table between us.

And this is where we came in.

'So, you've invented time travel.' I said, as if the proposition had been put to me a hundred times before; and maybe it had. I'd certainly read enough to recognise pseudo-scientific claptrap when I heard it. I'd met guys like this on lots of occasions, graduates who'd majored in applied physics and Dr Who and bombed in both. Or who'd never got further than GCSE and had completed their studies via Wikipedia. Perhaps I'm a little cynical – it goes with the territory - but in my book, you'll never get egg on your face if you steer clear of the chickens.

'Not invented, no,' said the fella, appraising me more carefully. 'Harnessing would be a better way to put it. Time is really a single continuous state of existence. What I've learned to do is tune in to an access point,' and he reached over to the device on

The ocean of sky

the table and touched a button.

'An access point?'

'Yes, an entryway to a new temporal location.'

'Time travel,' I repeated, with a sneer, aware that by confirming his definition I might also appear to endorse the proposition. I decided to pull his strings a little more firmly. 'So, have you travelled from the future to attend this jamboree?'

He smiled and did that thing with his glasses. 'No, and that's the just the point – it's only possible to travel back as far as the moment when the field generator is turned on.'

'Say again.'

'You can't travel back any further than the time at which you enter the access point.'

'And how long does the access point remain viable?'

'So far, I've been able to maintain it for six-point-six-five minutes.'

'So that's the limit of your ability to travel through time?' I said scornfully. 'Six-point-six-five minutes into the past? I thought this discovery was of "huge significance".'

He smiled again, only this time it was a brighter, more expansive smile.

'You don't remember me, do you? I could have dispensed with the glasses – they weren't much of a disguise anyway. But then, you're the sort of arrogant sod who ruins people's lives and forgets they ever existed.'

I frowned. Now I looked at him more closely there was something vaguely familiar; the hair was shorter perhaps and without the spectacles... Yee

Point of entry

God's! It was that little turd who I'd turned over in the article for The Daily News. "Government funded project wastes million in tax payers' money!"

'You're the chancer who spent wads of cash on a hairbrained scheme to...to...' I hesitated; the exact nature of the venture escaped me, but I remembered that it had involved some wholly unrealistic project which had wasted enough to pay off the National Debt! The Minister who endorsed it had got the chop after the story went viral and, now I thought about it, so too had the research team involved.

'Ahhh!' I let out a long breath as realisation came to me. 'You're the plonker who was running the show. Well, don't expect me to show sympathy, mate. As far as I'm concerned, you got what was coming. Don't tell me you're still trying to advance your madcap ideas. Bloody time travel now, is it? And you really thought I might give you a leg up? On your way sunshine! And take that damn Meccano-kit toy with you,' and I waved derisorily at the gizmo.

'You're right,' he said, pushing himself up from the armchair and stretching long arms, 'Six-point-six-five minutes isn't long but I've managed to build in a continuous loop to maintain the connection. I think you'll find it instructive.' And with that he turned and strode off towards the lobby.

I shrugged inwardly and picked up my brandy. Another member of the lunatic fringe. If I had a hot meal for...

The abandoned machine bleeped, once.

The ocean of sky

'So, you've invented time travel.' I said, as if the proposition had been put to me a hundred times before; and maybe it had. I'd certainly read enough to recognise pseudo-scientific claptrap when I heard it. I'd met guys like this on lots of occasions: graduates who'd majored in applied physics and Dr Who and bombed in both. Or who'd never got further than GCSE and had completed their studies via Wikipedia. Perhaps I'm a little cynical – it goes with the territory - but in my book, you'll never get egg on your face if you steer clear of the chickens.

Printed in Great Britain
by Amazon